Rembert Block

About the Author

ALEX SHAKAR is also the author of the critically acclaimed novel *The Savage Girl*. A Brooklyn native, he now lives in Chicago, Illinois.

CITY IN LOVE

Also by Alex Shakar

The Savage Girl

CITY IN LOVE
The New York Metamorphoses

Alex Shakar

Perennial

An Imprint of HarperCollins*Publishers*

The author gratefully acknowledges the help and support of James Michener, the Texas Center for Writers, the University of Texas Department of English, Zulfikar Ghose, Peter LaSalle, Elizabeth Harris, James Magnuson, Brad Engelstein, Hilary Liftin, Blue Montakhab, Damon Osgood, Aaron Roston, Shakars (Greg, Diane, Martin, Mary), The Group (Ehrstin, Ford, Skibell, Smith, Walsh).

Illustrations: pp. 92, 93, 97, 99, 101 by Lee Deigaard; p. 98 from *Violator*, Issue #3, Image Comics, Anaheim, CA, © 1994; p. 94 by the author.

This book was originally published in 1996 by FC2, Fiction Collective Two. It is here reprinted by arrangement with Fiction Collective Two.

HarperCollins books may be purchased for educational, business, or sales promotional use. For information please write: Special Markets Department, HarperCollins Publishers Inc., 10 East 53rd Street, New York, NY 10022.

First Perennial edition published 2002.

Designed by David A. Dean

Library of Congress Cataloging-in-Publication Data is available.

ISBN 0-06-050883-3

02 03 04 05 06 RRD 10 9 8 7 6 5 4 3 2 1

to O

CONTENTS

N.Y.C.
1 B.C.

THE SKY INSIDE

Lunatic Leaves Letter on Times Square

Screen, Egg on Finest's Faces!

H is the letter fixed in the mind of an unknown insane man, and on the face of the Jumbotron television screen, and now, in the imaginations of millions of New Yorkers.

It happened hours before dawn on the morning of March 4. The nimble symbolist climbed onto a billboard scaffold attached to the narrow face of One Times Square and hoisted it to the Jumbotron. Then, putting the available equipment to use, he painted on the screen a twelve foot-high letter H in billboard paste.

"He looked deranged," said a limousine driver who wishes to remain anonymous. "The static electricity from the screen made his hair rise up around his baseball hat."

The crazy character was not finished!

He raised the scaffold above the Jumbotron, up to the flashy Glitterati Magazine sign. He then smashed a hole into the bottom of the "Glitterator" — the giant glass tube which circulates an air-blown stream of glitter around the display. The glitter poured down the building and stuck to the glue, leaving a glittering H on the Jumbotron.

Meanwhile, in the Times Square police station — the one-story outpost located at the foot of the building — officers on duty remained unaware of the mayhem of littering, glittering and lettering going on right over their heads.

Unimpeded, the loony letter-setter lowered himself to the sidewalk and sauntered off!

The men in blue are red in the face, sources confide. They are checking mental wards for escapees, but have no substantial leads.

"There is not enough information to determine whether his delusions are those of paranoia, of grandeur, of persecution, or of reference," criminal psychologist Edward Leech admitted. "In this city, there are as many insanities as people!"

Maria

One time before I gone down to First Street to see Señora Menski. That was when my grandfather was sick and I did not know what for them to do, the healing or the death. So I gone to Señora Menski and she did the horoscope and she told me. My abuelo was going to die. I come back and they do the ceremony? and he died and he was happy.

But that day of the second time something happened and I did not know what it means. Because I was down in Mommy's basement dusting the altars? And I looked up through the small window in front and I saw them walking on the sidewalk. A China man and a China woman, and they was walking toward each other, walking real slow like, and they was both young like me, and they had I swear to God the same face, real calm, and wise. And they was crossing by each other without a word, without even a look. They was crossing by on the square of sidewalk right in front of my window and they keep on going, the same steps, touching the sidewalk at just the same times, like they was the two of them the same. I never saw any Chinese on my street and now there was two of them, crossing like that? I could not get them out of my head. It was a sign.

Signs are everywhere. They are more of them now then ever, signs giving birth to signs. I was not so good yet at reading them. So I gone down to Señora Menski to ask her what could this sign mean.

You know Señora Menski? *Madame* Menski. It say that on the window sign. She's real like funny looking? She be all big and fat with a face like bread dough and she got the one long hair sticking out of her chin and she wears the long dresses like so long you can't even see her feet? I know she don't look real wise and she don't talk real wise, but she's a wise lady and she knows the future even. So I asked her. And she drawed the lines on the maps with stars. And she measured with all the tools and scientific things. And she did the math. And she's like

Maria, yuh gonna find a *man*.

That's how she talk like.

I said I don't think so.

And she's like Why not. Yuh young and pretty. And powerful.

She said powerful. Just like they was always telling me at the centro, and she said the same thing.

I said Because I think, men are scared of me? Sometimes I got the temper. Men, they get all scared about that. Then they hear about my Spiritism and they think I am a brujera, a witch. They think that I am going to like put a hex on them or something.

And Señora Menski's face get all small and crafty and she's like, Them guys aint worthy a yuh. This time yuh gonna get a winner.

So I asked her What kind of man will he be. And she's like

Aquarius.

Then I am like But how will I meet him. How will I know.

But she just pours herself some tea and takes a little drink, this bitty little teacup in the middle of her big round head. I keep on trying for her to look at me? but she always looking at something else. The woman is crafty like that.

Then the door opens and this guy was coming in. So big he be bending down, like the whole world is all too small for him. He got these eyes? blue and real sleepy, and he's just standing there with the door open and his big jaw open, looking at me.

Señora Menski said Close the door Howie yuh letting in the cold. And he does it, and with this guy inside, the room all the sudden looked like tiny. His hands was real big and red and clumsy like big red tarantulas, and one tarantula goes up to this tiny baseball hat? three or four sizes too small for his head at least with this bitty letter *o* sewed on it with the wrong color thread. And he takes it off and shakes his shaggy head, lots of hair, not even blond: white. I know he sounds funny but he was real nice looking, and his sleepy eyes, and he and me just looking at each other. I could feel the spirits floating all around him. Some of them was going at him and others was protecting him. I thought, He is powerful. When he go to brush the hair out of his eyes, the spirits jump out of the way and spin around and then they come back down and sit on his big shoulders like little birds. He looked so gentle, like Santo Francis Ifá, god of impossible things and palm trees. I thought, I could trust this guy. Then he starts talking to me. And the way that he talks is so beautiful you could cry. And I thought, I could love this guy even.

Señora Menski asks me to me to keep her son company while she makes the dinner. So I'm staying for dinner. Just like that.

She is a crafty woman, that one. I ask him what sign is he? ...and what do you think....

Madame Menski

Who was Howard's father? I'm not gonna tell you. Because it's a secret, and that secret will stay with me to my grave. And when I'm dead, the secret's gonna bloom into a mystery. Like a caterpillar hiding away in its cocoon until it comes out a butterfly.

But I can tell you how I met him.

I never did meet him.

Aint that a riot.

Story of my life. See, when I was a little girl I had this thing for I don't know two three guys but I was never that lovely and they got away from me. Then there was this other guy but he died in a plane crash not when he was on the plane but when the plane crashed on him. But anyway, I knew that was my Fate. Cause everybody's got a Fate they can't do nothing about it's just like that. You got your fate all round you like a cloud of flies. You bat-at you bat-at it it don't go away. Still there, always been that way even before you were born. But anyway to get on with the story. I aint had a lotta luck with men. That was all right with me though cause most men aint worth the trouble and I got along fine without them thank you very much.

Except one thing. I needed a baby.

I needed a baby so it could be born on the day when the planets Mercury, Venus, Mars, Saturn, and Jupiter, plus the moon would all have a meeting in the house of Aquarius. Something like that comes around only once in two thousand years. I read that anybody who was born on that day would be like Superman. All the astrologers agreed. A new race of heroes were gonna be born that day.

I wanted a kid like that. I wanted a kid like that more than anything. Because I knew that heroes were exactly what this city needed. Because this city's like one of them books that's too big for anybody to read. It's got all these big words. It's got like millions of pages. And the story it tells don't seem to make sense. Some people pretend like they know what's going on. Other people just figure it's a bunch of crap. Other people feel stupid cause they don't understand. None of them's happy about it. But a hero would know the story. He'd know it like them speed reading guys can read a page just by looking at it. And he'd make everybody understand. Because they don't gotta read the book no more all they gotta do is look at the hero and then they understand. A hero is something everybody can understand. A hero is something you can sink your teeth into.

I decided to pick a man. I was awful naive back then. I figured I'd find a good one and lead him on plenty but I wouldn't give him none until the time was right, until it was right exactly nine months before the day of Aquarius so I could maximize my odds. That way I'd have plenty of time to check him out and make sure I got a good specimen. I figured to be a superman you gotta have good genes too.

See, I thought I could be picky. Cause I had a fresh supply of men coming through my place of work every day. That's right, fresh every day like salmon swimming up the stream to spawn. Cause...well, I was working in a bank.

Special kind of bank.

You get it yet?

For Sperm. I was working in a sperm bank and these men were coming in all ready to make their gift that keeps on giving. So I figured I could pick out a man and then use my wiles on him when he was in a pent-up state and whatnot.

Now I know what you're thinking. You're thinking Hey wait a minute. Lady's working in a sperm factory all she's gotta do is just take one of them test tubes and one of them injector thingees and bam pop goes the weasel. But I didn't want to have a baby like that. It wasn't natural. You go against Nature, Nature comes right back against you. That's the way it is. You don't believe it you got another thing coming.

So I tried to find a man. I tried for weeks but I didn't get nowheres. One I was too choosy and Two I was too shy. I tried to give them a little wink but they just got all embarrassed. Probably thought I was laughing at them cause they were going to be touching themselves in a minute. Finally it got down to the last couple days and I got nervous. I tried to get every man that day and they all went wrong, every single one of them. One guy's too busy, another guy's too tired, next guy's got some problem with live women, and that's the way it went. Until the last guy. He was kind of pale and his hands were sort of shaky, but it was a quarter to five and he was like I said the last guy in the place. I gave him the wink and he said to me,

Excuse me, but you got something in your eye?

I shook my head no.

He said, Well, you should get that tic checked out, they got hypnotists take care of that stuff now days.

I knew I had him when I offered to buy the drinks. We went to this bar and he drank all night long. I says Don't forget you gotta keep your end of the deal so don't get too drunk to you know. And he says, Madam you're dealing with a gentleman and a gentleman don't never louse on his agreements. And he orders another drink. I knew he was a drunk, but I wasn't too worried cause he was a regular donator so I figured he could rise to the occasion. He had these eyes that reminded me of a pirate because one eye had all these red veins like a grasping hand and the other was sleepy and cold like a hook. I started to like those eyes. He was a repossessor. Cars and stuff. I liked the sound of that. Repossessor. Goes and takes things back. I thought about that. Lot of things need taking back. He must feel like that.

We didn't get back to my place until six thirty in the morning, and the sun was coming up and the light over my bed was shaped like a fish and I stared at the light while he did it and it hurt but it was done quick and then he was out the door.

There was no way I could sleep so I went to work. I'd heard anyway that if you move around the sperms got a better chance of getting to the egg cause they get swished around like. So I was sitting behind the counter, bouncing my leg, trying not to think about how the repossessor had run out the door like that, when this guy like you would not believe comes in. He's got this golden hair and this build like one of them old statues of the astrology gods.

This was the guy I'd been waiting for. I knew it right off. I sure screwed up, I was thinking. Here I went and panicked and took some lousy drunk when meanwhile Fate had got this perfect man all lined up for me.

But then I thought, wait a minute. You can't never change your Fate. Your Fate is all written out for you like a book. It's written on your palms, in your dreams, in the cracks of the sidewalks, in the planets and the stars.

So I realized it might not be too late. The Sperms of the drunk repossessor were probably drunk too. They were probably weaving all over the road, crashing into each other, running out of gas, getting pulled over for reckless driving. And even though I wasn't anymore, my egg was maybe still a virgin.

And so I waited outside the booth while this guy inside was making his donation. And when he was done I took the cup from him and I got one of them syringes we used to put the sperms in the test tubes and I went into the ladies room and shot them up into me. I still felt like it was unnatural, but that morning I didn't know what was natural. With the repossessor sure didn't feel like natural.

Lot of times I think about what it would've been like if the beautiful man and me did it the natural way. I think about him a lot. I used to anyway. Sometimes I talk to him like he was around. He's my husband in a way, even though he don't even know I exist. I'm not gonna tell you who he is cause that's the secret. Those days, he wasn't nobody famous, but now days you'd have heard of him.

He was a very healthy man so it wasn't surprising that his little fishes caught up with the repossessor's little fishes, though actually, of course, it was a draw.

Chang

All time Howard sneak in to see show. He come in through East door and sit down low so no body notice. Soon he start to sit near me, and when I do show, some time he looking up watching all the star and other time he watching me doing control. Some time we talk and I say to him you should be at your post, you could get fire, and he nod but he don't move. Howard suppose to be guarding African Mammal but he say he like Planetarium better. Some time he sit there two, three show in a row, and he must been very lucky cause no body ever notice.

So he was there low down in shadow when museum director come in to tell me next year they make control automated and my job will be obsolete. Seventeen year I doing control. I had plan retire in three year. He say now I retire in nine month. He act like I should be happy and I act like I am happy. I think I am happy but when director leave and I see Howard looking at me, I get tear in my eye. You not interested about me I know but you want to know about Howard and I think this say some thing about him. Sure he crazy maybe but he could see thing too, and he care so truly.

He come up to me with sad face and put his arm on my shoulder and say, Come on Mister Chang, we go get drink now. I shut down console and we leave. It is hot day but he wear long trench coat and hat with letter *a* low down over his eye, and I ask why he dress like that and he confess he don't like his guard uniform. I ask where we going and he say "Doubling House." Yes, that is place, but he say "Doubling" because you go there to be doubling your vision.

It is OK bar. We stay there for many hour. Howard is big man and he drink four beer for every one I drink but I am not used to drink, and I think I get drunk as him. He talk four times much as me too.

About what? Lot of thing. One thing was this. He tell me to think about city. Think about city hard as you can. Try to see it all at once in your mind. Try to see every thing from deepest underground pipe and wire and foundation block to tallest peak and every thing in between. Try to see it from every angle, from north and east and south and west and all the view from every window inside it and from every eye of every person, where they live and where they go and what they do and how they feel about it too.

I can't do way Howard talk. He talk in really quite beautiful way.

So he tell me to think about all this and I do it for long time. We both sitting with two finger at our head like this. Then bartender come over and ask what we do, and Howard tell him same thing he tell me, and bartender try to think too and so all three of us there with two finger like this.

After while I look up, and Howard ask me what do I think. And I say, I don't know, nothing. And I think some more and I say, it seem funny. He ask why, and I say, It seem ridiculous. May be I say that because I was drunk and every thing seem ridiculous. After all, I am man of science. But bartender get very excited and say that is what he think too, that it is all wrong, that it is not as it should be, that he smell bloody rat in it some where.

And Howard nod his head.

And bartender ask Howard Why it is I smell rat?

And Howard say, Because, just as you say, it is all wrong, and in their most deepest most secretest soul, every body know it.

It is hard for me to say how serious is Howard. I know I have problem some time with people to tell how serious are they. Some time people being sarcastic and I don't see. I take every thing serious. So may be he pull on my leg, or may be he just drunk. But if you ask me, I tell you, Howard seem very serious to me. And very sad. Some thing trouble him. Some big thing. Thing does not seem right to him. He smell rat in it.

We keep drinking and I don't remember much until we leave bar. By that time was late at night and I remember bright place where we eat pizza and drink another beer. And then we walk again and next thing that I know we are at back door of museum and Howard open it with his key. I tell you now; I don't care because even if you tell, they can't do any thing to me now. Beside, we did no harm.

He go to closet and get two flashlight and we walk around dark museum very quiet. We keep away from lobby where night guard stay. We walk through forest section, shining our light on all the tree. We walk through Howard's section, African

Mammal, and Howard stare at lion for long time with head and both hand up against glass. He seem very angry there, angry at glass. I think he about to break through to get to lion, and I put my hand on his shoulder and lead him away.

In Hall of Mineral we charge all the fluorescent mineral with our flashlight, opal and nadorite, fluorite, wernerite, calcite, and we turn off flashlight and watch them glowing green blue red orange like frozen bit of sea and sky and sun. And we sneak through all the Ancient People, looking at all the Amazonian with painted body, and fierce Berber, and Mongolian in their helmet and suit of armor. We walk through Hall of Human Biology with people split open down middle and family of skeleton sitting in living room watching television set.

Most people do not know science. They do not know how any thing work. They do not know how television work or how mineral work or how human being work. I am always amaze at this. But this night I do not think as man of science. And I am scare. It all seem beautiful or crazy, I do not know which.

We walk under big blue floating whale, and over to other whale, sperm whale being squeeze by giant squid, and we walk through Hall of Meteorite, with all the space rock full of hole from traveling million of mile. We spend long time looking at skeleton of dinosaur, shining circle of flashlight slowly over all the bone, starting from tail and slowly up and up so with every bone we are more and more amaze, and head so high above. Then we sneak into Planetarium and shine our light into display of what happen if Sun make Earth three degree hotter or colder, New York under water, New York bury in white ice. And I stand on Mercury scale and I say Hey I weigh fifty pound! And Howard stand on Jupiter scale and say Hey I weigh seven hundred ninety two pound! And I think, that is where he belong, planet Jupiter, place where he weigh seven hundred ninety two pound.

Finally we go into Sky Theater, and I turn on Star Projector, and we lie down in aisle and stare up at all the star.

And he say, You know something wrong when you have to go inside building to see star at night. It is all ass on backward, he say, forest inside, jungle inside, sea inside, sky inside.

He seem to become sad, so I got to my console and turn on all the constellation, and all sudden, like magic, he is so excited, like little boy, and he make me tell him all their name, what is that one, and that one, and I sit over him like father telling bed time story, and may be I would have made a good father, because in little while Howard fell to sleep.

Terrorist Maims Main, Soaks Street!

Rats and water flooded Rivington Street yesterday morning in what may be the beginning of a new wave of urban terror! Investigators discovered the water main had been cut with a hacksaw in several places. It was an "expert job," sources say.

After the water drained, workers spotted a letter "r" painted on a nearby manhole cover. Police are investigating the possibility that this and other acts of vandalism involving letters of the alphabet in recent months are the work of a single man, representing an organization of unknown origin and size.

Who is he? What does he want? These are the questions authorities are scrambling to answer.

"We are not sure what brand of terrorist we're dealing with. He could very well be a Muslim, perhaps a Campesino, a card-carrying Union Member, or even a Syndicalist. We must consider even the most frightening possibilities," said criminal psychologist Anthony Scrima.

Local building owners are reporting property damage, and shop owners are claiming loss of inventory from basement flooding. But others see a bright side to the act.

"At least the streets got cleaned for once," said local tenant Roberto Diaz. "And it sure took care of the rats!"

Madame Menski

d raw. Yeah, that's what I said. It was a draw. I had twins.

At first I thought the beautiful man had won big, cause both of them was such bright little guys, with white hair and eyes the color of kiddy pools, this clear blue that made you want to cry to look at. But after a month, Gus's eyes turned brown and his hair got darker until it was dark as his eyes, and then I knew he was the repossessor's kid.

Day of Aquarius turned out to be the easy part. See, in them nine months I'd done a lot of studying. I'd learned all about the science of astrology. I wanted to be ready to read all the signs in the right ways, so I would know what to do when the time came to do it. I wanted to be a good mother for my superbabies. You can't change Fate, but I figure maybe you can help it along. So I studied day and night. I learned math so I could figure all the angles. I learned about the gravity effects from the planets on human beings. I learned about the astrology gods and the wisdom of the ancients. And what I learned told me that things weren't so simple like I'd thought.

You might not have known this, but the hour and even the minute you're born in can make you a different person. So turns out not only I was shooting for February fourth, the day of Aquarius, but nine at night, when the sun would be in Aquarius too, all lined up with the planets.

But my babies started trying to get out too soon—noon on February third. I was so upset. I'd come so close. I was screaming from the pain and crying from the sadness. And my neighbor heard me and she came down and called an ambulance.

In the hospital I tried to explain it to the doctor that for astrological reasons my babies couldn't be born until tomorrow. I figured they probably had some kind of drug to keep them in there till tomorrow night. I was trying to sound rational but I was in pain and screaming and I guess he thought I was hysterical or something. He said something about liability and told me there wasn't nothing they were gonna do to stop my babies from coming out whenever they felt like it.

They wheeled me into a little room and they put my legs up in them things they got just to embarrass you. And then the doctor was standing over me saying Push Push. And I screamed out at him, saying

Don't you order me around Mister Doctor. What, you forget how to treat a lady or didn't they teach you that in your doctor school.

And then the doctor started screaming back at me, getting all hysterical on me, like he's the one's got the belly full of aches and babies.

It went on and on. Them doctors and nurses saying Push! Push!

And me saying

Unnh! Unnh!

trying to hold them in, and thinking Come on Fate I aint gonna change you I'm just gonna help you out a little just a little while longer.

That lasted for fifteen hours. It was three in the morning on February fourth when little Gus came out screaming and crying. Which meant his rising sign was Taurus. Not good news. First cause Taurus is an earth sign and Aquarius is an air sign and the two of them just don't mix. And Second, the house of Taurus was badly aspected, which means it was coming at them planets at this wicked angle. All the planets wouldn't be helping my little Gus. They wouldn't be standing up and fighting him neither. But they would be tripping him up all the time, and he'd never see them do it. They would blindside him every time, and my poor baby'd never know what hit him.

And that was the good news, that day. Howie stayed inside six more hours. They said he was too big to come out the normal way and I'd bled so much blood they had to wait long as they could before they cut me open to get him out.

But when they were ready, I realized what time it was and I begged them to let him stay inside for longer. They told me he'd die. I begged them, explaining

He don't want to come out yet He knows what he's doing He'll come when he's good and ready.

Then I blacked out. *They* blacked me out is what happened. They cut him out of my womb at nine in the morning. Rising sign Leo. Head on against Aquarius and all them powers — the moon, Mars, Venus, Mercury, Saturn, Jupiter. They'd all be dead set against him and he'd have to fight the whole gang of them.

But at least he would recognize his enemies. His Leo was a fire sign and would light the way. Make him strong too. And those genes wouldn't hurt neither.

Yeah, Howie was so special. I knew it long before all the sports trophies and school awards. He was the one who could guide us all. He was telling me how to change my life even from back when he was two years old. It was their second birthday and I was icing him and Gus's cake. I went to check on them and I saw Howie sitting by the coffee table and he had all these slashes all over him, these red slashes, and I screamed, but even as I was screaming I was seeing that it was only lipstick. He'd got into my purse and spilled everything out of it. All the dollars and all the checks he'd torn up and chewed up and even ate some I bet. And one of my star charts I left out he scribbled on with the lipstick. But when I took a closer look, it was incredible. His scribble made this brand new constellation. Two eyes made from little groups of stars and then a mouth. The mouth began at Castor's head. Castor is the taller one of the two Gemini twins. The line went from there to the other twin Pollux and then kept going straight on through the body of Cancer and all the way to Regulus, in the Leo constellation. If he stopped the line there the mouth would have been sad. But he didn't want that. The line curved up, and there was no star there so he just drew one in, a little red blob.

That day changed my life. Howie told me what to do. To get my baby twins to a happy place I needed to make my own star. Sure it's true I couldn't live without money, but Howie was right. I needed to tear up that way of living. I needed to take a chance. So I started doing horoscopes for people. I told people what was gonna happen and then it happened and they spread the word. Pretty soon, I opened up this little parlor. And all this cause Howie showed me the way when he was two years old.

There are a whole bunch of other stories I could tell you.

One thing I always knew. He was meant for something heroic.

Gus? Well, he was a special kid too, and I love him with all my heart, whatever he thinks of me. They were close at first, like twins should be. Howie was bigger and looked out for Gus. And Gus looked up to him like crazy. Gus was the older one, but Howie was the leader. Howie was always the star. When they were getting older, Gus started getting all resentful about Howie, resentful toward his brother and toward me too for all the love I gave Howie, all the talking I did about how special he was and all the special things he was gonna do. So maybe that was my fault.

But how could I help it. It was written in the genes and in the stars both. I tried to treat them the same, but Howie was so special, and Gus was such a sensitive boy. It aint easy following in Howie's footsteps.

Detective Menski

Monday mornings are the worst, what with the IN box thicker than the Yellow Pages. Used to live for the weekends but after a while I saw that weekends just made the whole thing worse, like torture routines where the guy gets nice for a minute, gives his victim a cigarette, just to resensitize him to the even nastier beatings to come, or like the good cop who pretends to reason just so the bad cop can do his very baddest. So after a while I was onto weekends, hip to their little game, so those rare times I risked going outside on some sunny day I made sure not to let down my guard. If I went to Central Park or something it was just another office, an office with grass and trees, and Sheep Meadow was just one big IN box full of grass-smokers and child molesters and pimps and embezzlers, the whole city was my IN box, what can I say?

Usually, Monday mornings it took me a while to brave the IN box. I'd sit in the front room at the fingerprinting table, drink my coffee. This one Monday morning I saw Mooney on his way out. I asked him where he was going.

New lead on Letterhead, he said.

They called him Letterhead. Letterhead pissed me off from the start. As if we didn't have enough hassles dealing with the crackheads and the cokeheads and the potheads and all those garden variety heads, some maladjusted geek had to go and make the city into a fuckin' crossword. Giant *H* on the Times Square Screen, right above a police station. Month later an *O* painted on the Statue of Liberty's book. At that point the thinking was political, H-O for Homeless maybe, unless he was just in it for laughs. Ho Ho Ho, the joke's on us, or Santa Claus drunk on eggnog in the off-season.

But a month later to the day a huge flag showed up on the Manhattan-side archway of the Brooklyn Bridge. *W.* The Homeless thinkers thought Letterhead messed up and got it upside-down, but that was fantasy, they just couldn't stand being wrong. Next month, an *a* made of sheet metal, ten feet high, slapped on with Krazy Glue or something to the wall of Carnegie Hall. Couldn't get it off. Had to chisel out the damn wall. Odd thing *there* was, it was lowercase, and going back to the others we realized that the O and the W could be lowercase too, whatever that was worth. Next one showed up on Rivington, a letter *r* spraypainted on the street right above the spot he'd sawed through a water pipe and flooded the street. That's when the stakes got raised. Yeah, sure, it was more serious, but that's not what I mean. I mean literally, the stakes around here, I mean the betting pool here in the precinct. Every flatfoot getting into detective work, winner-take-all: **How are you NY? How are you going to stop me? How are the little fetuses going to defend themselves?** and etcetera, and I got so sick of it I stopped paying attention. Just what Letterhead wanted, a roomful of cops thinking about him day and night, just what he had wet dreams about. He wasn't going to get *me* playing his game. It wasn't my concern. Why does anybody do what anybody does? This city gets bigger and taller and hairier by the day, like a baby gorilla. It gets bigger and hairier and people get weirder and weirder about it, start to panic, beat their heads like bongos, paint their asses blue and dance around bonfires. If they could make you think about why they were doing it, you'd go nuts too. Worst ones were the ones that made you think. I tried to avoid those.

I said So what's it this time, Mooney? Did he bend the Twin Towers into an X?

Mooney told me, the sidewalks. Got a description this time. From a couple garbagemen. Guy wearing an M hat, capital M, big backpack, probably full of paint, with tubes coming out of it and down his pants, big contraption on his shoes with sponges on the bottom, making purple footprints. Guess is, he was spelling out one big M all over the island. He was crossing the street when the garbage truck came barreling down on him, you know how those assholes drive at night, and Mister M not only doesn't get out of the way, he just stands there, the truck guys honking and stepping on the brakes. Last second, motherfucker jumps out of the way. Then, jumps onto the side of the truck and rips off one of the chrome horns that's still blaring at him. Then he runs away.

He tried to hand me the report but I waved it off. I said M, eh. So what's your theory now? *How are Marshmallows Made? How are My Relatives on Mars?*

We're way past all that, he said. Didn't you hear about the *d*?

I hadn't.

Mooney told me. The lowercase *d* on the D trains. Motherfucker changed the signs on all the D trains. From big D to little d....

I still didn't get it. I said That's nice Mooney. I'm real happy for you.

But then he said The *d*, which makes it *Howard. Howard M* now, if this lead checks out.

I remember then half my donut fell into the drink and I stared at it glazed and bobbing hunched-over like a drowned man. Mooney was spouting new theories, something about him being an artist, promoting himself. Something about the city's growing artist infestation problem. Cockroaches, rats and artists, blah blah... and meanwhile me thinking No, it couldn't be, it couldn't.

I said, So...what's the description, Mooney?

Mooney gave me some shit for being curious all of a sudden. I let him have his laugh.

Six foot nine, he tells me. Three hundred pounds. All muscle.

I felt like I was going to vomit. I don't think I let it show.

I said That's all, Mooney? No hair color, eye color, skin color?

White guy.

For a minute I got paranoid, thinking why'd he say White guy, why not Caucasian, thinking maybe Mooney was already way ahead of me, maybe he had it all figured out and was baiting me, seeing if I knew. But that passed. This was Mooney we're talking about. I said, That's not much, Mooney.

It's something, he said, a little offended-like, and I knew he was in the dark. Besides, maybe I was wrong, always that chance.

I said, Listen, Mooney, I think the fresh air would do me some good. You mind if I tag along with you?

He said What fresh air.

That IN box, you know, Monday mornings...

He said sure.

Maria

Evil thoughts get spread just like a material, physical disease. They get spread through the air from one person to the other. They get spread by wicked spirits, the muertas who are in darkness, who have not been bring to the light. It's hard to tell them from the good spirits, the protectors and the guides. Even sometimes they can be disguising like the saints. I thought I could tell them from the other. That was arrogance. I paid the price.

My centro was not a good centro. There was all sorts of jealousy and the Padrino didn't care. All the other godchildren was envying my progress. My first time I felt funny all over. I started to laugh. And then I was crying. When the Padrino hit me with the bandanna, I wanted to dance. I wanted to jump up and down. I felt hot and cold. And then I don't remember, but when I was waking up I was on the floor and the white table was turned over and the bowls of water was broken and the mediums was holding me down. In only three months the Padrino was making me a medium and I was starting to sit at the table? and the godchildren and the mediums could not understand about my progress.

One night after the meeting, Altagarcia come up to me and was like, Maria, where is your Blanco. My Blanco is what they called Howard because he was white and his hair was light. Altagarcia is like, Why he never picks you up at night, this neighborhood is no good for a girl alone. Altagarcia was a medium at the table. She never even talked to me before but now she was all like putting her arm around me? and I told her that Howard worked real hard.

That is not so funny for the boyfriend not to come to the centro. Most boyfriends? they don't believe in the Spiritism or they are scared of it and they don't want nothing to do with it. Howard was not like that. He loved me he said because I am going out every day and I am reading the city like a book. He said that was the thing that people needed. The city needed the reading. People needed the reading to. So he was supporting, but he did not believe that the Spiritism could work for him. Maybe he was hoping for me to teach him. But he never come to the centro.

Altagarcia give me this look like she was sorry for me. She said the spirits was telling her things about my Blanco, and she said when I am ready, she could tell me and she could help me do what could be done.

I tried not to show it, but that made me start thinking. Howard come home real late that night. He was doing that like all the time. He told me he was at work. He told me he worked late in the museum? But I did not believe that any more.

If only he told me the truth. Maybe if only I asked him he could have told me. But we still did not know each other real good and we loved each other but we was still real shy. We made love with the lights turned off, and we took off our clothes in the bathroom or under the covers. You know, I had like only once seen him all the way naked? I see him now standing there: he was so big and strong but he was so white and helpless like a baby. If only I trusted more. But I couldn't get what Altagarcia said out of my head.

My day off of work I was at home watching TV. And on the show there was the man who was being not faithful to the wife, and the man and the wife was in the living room, and he was lying to her. I saw that in the living room there was this lamp. The bottom part was like a statue of a man holding up the light and the shade in his arms. It was the same lamp in our living room, that Howard had find in the trash and bring home. The one on TV was green? and ours was blue? but besides that, they was the same. I should have paid attention to how the colors was different, but to me it looked like proof. Signs are everywhere. But signs are like the mbua with the hundred heads. Only one of them got the brain. But all of them got teeth, and all of them bite.

I cried out loud. I picked up the lamp and I smashed it on the floor.

When he come home I leaved the TV turned on. He hated the TV. His hands gone up to his head and he leaved the room? and that was to me like more proof. I gone into the bedroom and I asked him when we was going to be married and he look at me with his sleepy eyes that I trusted so much and he told me never in this lifetime. And he told me that I needed to be finding another man.

The next week I went to Altagarcia. I said, my husband got another woman. And she smiled and was like, she knew it already, the saints was telling her that. She said for three hundred dollars there was something we could do.

The next few nights we did the sacrileges. I can't believe I was part of that. But I got the temper. I got it real bad that time. I got it so bad that I did not see the signs and I did not understand what me and Altagarcia was doing until the third night.

The first night we killed a black cat. We killed it real slow. We tied up the legs and cut it and burned it with knives and matches, and then we put it in a big pot and boiled it. I won't never forget how that cat was screaming. Altagarcia went to the cemetery and buried it. And I gone home and it was already the morning and I had all the cuts from the cat claws and I gone to bed and I was having nightmares all day long.

The second night she gone and digged the cat back up. We boiled it again with the grave dust and the garlic and pepper in the same pot. Altagarcia put some rum in her mouth and spit it in the pot and then lighted a cigar and blowed the smoke inside. Then she gone away with the pot, back to the cemetery. After the second night I gone home different. I was thinking about the things we was doing but I was not feeling anything. I was thinking about Altagarcia's apartment, about the black candles and the little frogs hopping in the jars on the shelf, and the black chicken. This was not Spiritism, this was Santería. I knew that. But I did not care.

The third night she asked me to bring something of Blanco's, some clothing. I brought his baseball cap that he put the letters on. One time I asked him what the letters means and he told me it was something that was doing with astrology, but I did not believe that anymore? and so I choosed the baseball cap because it was another secret and I hated it and I wanted to tear it to pieces.

That night Altagarcia put different things on the table. She put a bag of earth from the cemetery wrapped up in a black rag. She put a jar with holes in the metal top and inside the jar was a caterpillar making a cocoon. She lighted a church candle, and heated up a tail of a scorpion. Then she took out the caterpillar and stuck the scorpion tail through its little head, and she was saying

Changó he he gue gue ha mayo Changó enkanga mbua

I shouted out

Altagarcia, no!

It's funny that when we boiled the cat I did not know. But when I saw the caterpillar stick to the table and going this way and that way in pain, then I knew. This is not only the Santería, this is the brujería, this is the black magic.

She looked at me. Probably she could not believe I did not know before.

She told me take the earth from the cloth and rub it on the inside of the hat. That was the only thing needing to do now. I could have not did it. But I did.

So it was my fault what happened to Howard, all of the pain. I could have did the good magic, the healing. I did the evil magic instead.

I will never forgive myself, but Howard forgives me. I know it from the spirits. And I know it from what he did. What he did showed the way. What he did give me so much pain, but the more I thought, the more beautiful that it was. It made me see that I was going on the dangerous path, and I was all caught up in the evil thoughts. I am at a new centro now, and it's a much better centro, it's got a Padrino who cares. In time, if the spirits are supporting, I will be the head medium, and I will use my powers to help people to understand the signs like people used to in the old times. Ay, yes, this is where I belong. If some day I leave the centro the saints are going to bring me back the hard way. Wherever I go, they are going to find me and they are going to bring me back the hard way. They are going to bring me back the hard way to the same place.

Letter Artist Waylays Wall Street —
Baffled brokers foot the bills!

n dollar bills covered the main trading floor of the New York Stock Exchange yesterday morning, in the latest "installation" from the letter artist's *œuvre*!

Tapes from security cameras show the maestro at work between 4:34 and 4:44 A.M. He wears spandex pants and a t-shirt and carries two satchels strapped across his shoulders. From the satchels, he scatters the bills — counterfeit dollar bills with the letter 'n' where the denomination would normally appear. His face is concealed by a bandanna and a baseball cap on which the letter 'n' can be seen.

The letter artist was caught on film, but not by police. The security guard on duty was asleep, sources confide.

Investigators believe the letter artist gained access to the Exchange disguised as a bicycle messenger in the late afternoon. He then hid somewhere in the building for the next twelve hours.

"The messenger disguise is not inappropriate," criminal psychologist Kenneth Byle explains. "The artist is a kind of messenger, from a place of symbols, allusions, illusions, where physical and moral laws do not apply."

At one point in the videotape, the artist appears to be in pain. He leans forward, his legs buckle and his hands clutch the sides of his head. Experts are not certain whether the agony is real, or part of a carefully choreographed performance.

Stockbrokers wandered the trading floor in confusion, picking up the bills and examining them. Investors were not amused by the funny money. The N.Y.S.E. composite index ended down 5.88 points at the closing bell.

Authorities are calling for calm. "There is no cause for alarm," Mr. Byle said. "We may rest assured that we — that the solid majority of us at any rate—are in no way vulnerable to the message of art. Because the messenger, eloquent as he may be, invariably speaks a language all his own."

Madame Menski

So where is he?

That's all he says. He aint come around for three years and that's all I get. I told him

I knew you'd be coming, Gus. Howie told me you'd be coming.

He was here? Gus says. And I tell him

Yes, Gus, Howard was here. But aint here now and he aint coming back.

Gus asked me if I knew what Howie was doing and I

says yes but I don't tell him nothing else. He says he's gotta turn Howie in. Even if he didn't want to, he'd have to, cause probably they already know. They're starting to avoid Gus at the police station. He says they're gonna get Howard with or without him.

They won't get my Howie, I says, and neither will you. He'll always be one step ahead of you.

That makes him mad. Gus didn't look good. His face was like one of them rubber masks of the politicians, with all them rubbery folds and holes for the real eyes and the real eyes look the most unnatural of all. I told him that and he snapped back something I don't remember what. No, I remember I just don't want to say it. Whore. Same thing as all the other times. Ever since I told them they had two different fathers. I never told him how his father the repossessor was the only man I actually... you know. But it's probably better him thinking of me like a natural whore than like a unnatural mother.

We didn't say anything for a while. Then he says

Why? Just tell me why Howard's doing this?

I shook my head.

Why? I just want to know.

I says,

You wouldn't understand, Gus, and you know it, so why bother?

I'm going to find him and throw him in jail, he says, looking just like a big fat cop but sounding just like a little boy.

I says,

He's dying, Gus.

I went to Howard's trophy shelf and got the X-ray. We looked at it together. I showed him the tumor, a thick, stringy cloud like the Milky Way in the middle of his head.

He asked me how long I'd known. Only since that afternoon. Howard came and gave me the x-ray. He was in constant pain, he told me, so much pain that half the time he felt like ripping out his eyes just to get rid of the pressure.

Do you know what a cancer is? Howie explained it to me. He said a cancer is little bits of everything all growing together without any sense. Little bits of bone and teeth and heart and spleen and finger and toenails and even little bits of brain, like a city, all those different things, all those shadows and sharp edges growing all cold and confused. There's a city growing inside his head, and it's killing him. He came, he said, to say goodbye.

He wants us to be a family again, I told Gus. Gus sat down, and said

Hell of a way to show it.

He wants the whole city to be a family again, I says.

His face was awful, like the rubber was beginning to melt. No, he wasn't crying, it was worse than that. I wasn't crying either. That just aint the way we do things around here.

What happened to him, Gus starts asking me. He says What happened What happened. What happened to Howard when we were kids. Why did he start changing like that. Why did he give up on everything. Why did he start hiding away in his room all the time. What happened to him. Just tell me.

I tell him

It was Fate Gus. Fate happened to him.

Gus looked at me like he aint never been more disgusted. He asked me again where was Howard.

He stares at me, them dark eyes. And I see my little boy again.

I just want to talk to him, he said. I promise. I just want to see him.

Chang

Kerosene. Yes. I bring kerosene when he ask. But most time I bring only food. I had to get for him. He could not be seen. Two detective already come ask me about him on two different day. At time I did not know where was Howard so I was not saying lie. He stop coming to work. I tell second detective one already come day before, and he was surprise. Later, Howard tell me first one his half-brother.

I find out where was Howard when he sneak into Sky Theater one day, after last show. He take me down into basement of museum where he hiding. It is large basement down there with many room and most of them just for storage of item from old exhibit. Some of these room no body see in year. So it was good hiding place. He bring me in to one room and lead me through maze of old dusty junk, bunch of display stand and pane of glass and sack of plaster and stuffed bird in plastic wrapping. And in back of there was space with some paint can and saw and hammer and piece of metal and food wrapping all over floor, and path leading through all that to corner where Howard had bunch of cloth for bed and little lamp and bunch of newspaper clipping.

He tell me I could look at clipping. He had done it, all the letter.

No, I did not need to ask. I look at these clipping, and I know. He tell me newspaper people will figure out it is him just like police, and they will come around too with question. All sort of people.

You did come. All of you with tape recorder and little pad of paper always scribble and scribble. I say nothing. Still you come. It is over now. Now I tell. You never get right. But not matter. Try and try. That is part of story too. You and you and you. Part of story.

So yes, I help. I come early to work every morning and go down to bring food and other thing he need. Yes. Kerosene. No. I did not know. Who can tell what he thinking, this guy inside? He seem very calm, even with pain in his head. I ask him Howard why you do this thing with all the letter and he look at me with blank face and he say

Do you have better idea some thing to do?

And I look at him with blank face and I say

No Howard I guess I do not. And I am thinking first time in my life I know sarcastic and I am sarcastic too and I laugh at joke we make. But his face still blank. I stop laughing. It is quiet and he look deep in to my eye and I feel all sudden cold chill.

And then, he start laughing, and then I laugh, and we both laugh.

Now I will tell you about the day Howard help me do the star.

My last day at work, Star Projector would not move. Motor was broken. It was bad for while and I already report problem but no body come to fix it and now it was broken. I go down to Howard with some cereal and milk and tell him there will be no show today. He was very upset about it. He know this is my last day. He say let people come in, and he will think of some thing.

At first I did not want to do it, but then I say to myself, they get rid of me anyway, what can they do to me? And so

I let people in for show. There was very big crowd that day. Lot of little school children on class trip, and family, and tourist come in and sit down and look up at dome and wait.

Just when show suppose to begin, Howard come in and walk down aisle and step up on to round platform of Projector. He stand up against base, with back of his neck under the crossbeam and arm wrap around each side, like holding up giant bar bell. He was big man, but under Star Projector he look so small. Light come from platform and he glow red and yellow and Projector glow over him purple and blue. And green light come from my console. And I see shadow head of all the audience turn and look to Howard, then to me, then to him again. He look at me, and I point my finger at north module and then point up. And he strain with all his power and his head is ram up against metal and turning very red, and I afraid he will break all his bone, but south end start to go down and north start to go up, and finally it is in place. And we do whole show like that. He look at me at my console, and I show where to move it, and he make it move. And when show was over, I turn up all the light and all the kid cheer, and all the grown-up cheer too, and Howard unwrap his two arm from Star Projector, and step forward, cover with perspiration, and he smile, and bow to audience. And I clap loudest of all.

Not long ago, I go to see his mother and we talk about Howard. I tell her how he had love the Sky Theater. And she show me constellation that he had draw, with extra star, and she told me how it had change her life. I said to her Howard had change all our life. He take all the city in his two hand, all the wild metal and glass and jumble of light, and he give it a human face.

More and more, I think not like man of science. But this no longer make me scare.

I will tell you what I did, because they take away my console and computer does my job so what can they do to me now? I go back to Sky Theater. I climb up on pedestal and unscrew one of the many lens of South module. I remove the slide. And with pin, I make tiny hole so light shine through in just right spot. So that now, when you visit Planetarium, if you know about such thing and you look to spot just off Regulus, you will perceive brand new star in night sky. And that is Howard's star. And for those who do not know about such thing, a child may be who just love the star and not know why, child with mind that is similar to mind of Howard, may be this child will see constellation, two eye and mouth that start out sad but then is happy after all, and may be he be console.

Detective Menski

Invitations. Like it was a party or something. Mine came express mail, on my desk in the afternoon. *You are cordially invited to the apotheosis of Howard Menski. Tonite. Eight. Atop the Empire State Building.*

I thought about telling Mooney. But I didn't. I'd be damned if the whole department showed up to laugh their fat asses off at my dysfunctional family.

I went to make the rounds. I didn't want to go by the station to get a car so I jumped in front of a cab and flashed my badge and told him First Street and step on it. My mother hadn't seen him, but she'd gotten an invitation. Same story with that chiquita banana of his. Beads and crosses all over that godforsaken Spanish Harlem tenement and that stink of incense that always brought back a bad taste in my mouth. Last two times I'd been there she'd done the No speaka de English with me, but now that he'd stopped coming home and she got the invite and she was scared, her language skills got a lot better, miracle of miracles. She even wanted to talk about various interpretations of the word apotheosis but I didn't have time for that. It meant something antisocial, that much I was sure of and that was enough for me.

The cabs kept taking off even though I told them to wait but that's no surprise; they all got twenty relatives to buy plane tickets to New York for and an expensive turban habit besides. I went to see that Chang character at the museum, and he was even more nervous than usual, let it slip he knew about my relation to Howard, so I knew he'd had contact. Which he admitted but he wouldn't talk and I didn't have the stomach for the normal threats of being an accessory to etcetera, what with him yapping

you-can-not-do-any-thing-to-me

over and over like water torture, and me thinking what the hell did Howard tell him about me?

I couldn't take anymore. I hailed a cab and and told him to get me to the best bar in the neighborhood, official police business. He took me to some upscale Irish joint. I sat down at the end and waited for the bartender. On the TV set there was that commercial for razorblades. That new thing they do. Guy's head mutates into another guy's head and so forth. Caucasoid, Negroid, Caucasoid, Mongoloid, Caucasoid, Caucasoid and on and on like a person's face doesn't mean anything. Every time I saw that commercial I got sick to my stomach. Is it too much to ask to be able to just stand up without some jerk yanking the rug from under you?

Meanwhile the bartender still hadn't come over. He was just standing there with his eyes rolled back and a finger pointed into each temple like he was running an electric current through his bean. I said

What the hell are you doing?

He shot me a dirty look and said

Whassa bloody matter lad ya never seen a man meditatin'?

I said

Oh *sorry* Mister O'Maharishi but I was wondering if you might perchance meditate me up a Manhattan

thinking what the hell, this whole city gone queer on me? But he knew his business and when I told him to keep them coming they kept coming at least. I wanted to sort things out in my head but I couldn't, I was too angry. I'd thought about it so much already and come up blank. Why had Howard thrown his life away? Back when we were kids I mean. He was so good at so many things, all those things where there are clear winners and clear losers, any sport that needed wrestling, running, throwing things, he could do all that. Anything they gave grades for, math, science, he was always at the top. My only guess was all those normal things stopped being a challenge for him. He got into weirder and weirder stuff. Psychology, religion, history, art, games so big you never know if you're winning or losing or just spinning your wheels. I don't know. Why does anybody do what anybody does? I thought my life would be clear cut, you know, good guys, bad guys. I had no idea.

I left at six thirty with enough booze in me to burn midtown to the ground. Yeah, I used to have that problem, drinking. I had the cab stop at a liquor store on the way. I was up on the observation deck early. I wanted to be there before Howard so that I could beat the shit out of him and drag his ass to jail before he could get his little party underway. How I wanted to beat him, just this once. How I wanted to save him.

There was no sign of him. I looked out at the city. It was cold and the wind was whipping around and there was snow, gray on the streets and white on the rooftops, but the sun was there too, going down, and red glare off all the windows. It was February fourth. He'd pulled his stunts the fourth of each month. Today was our birthday.

The three of them showed up. Maria, then Chang, and then just before nine my mother. I told them, Glad you could all make it here to see some police brutality, I'll do my very best to make it entertaining. Maria and Chang looked scared but my mother just snorted. She'd seen Howard pin me to the ground so many times she couldn't imagine the chips falling any different. But I'd learned a couple tricks since then, taken down guys just about his size, and I wasn't even angry then.

But I wasn't prepared for the way he came up onto the roof. She was right, our mother. He was one step ahead. A big glass jug strapped onto his back, full of kerosene, I could smell it. A tube coming out the bottom, taped along his back and down his arm. A cloth wick sticking out the end of the tube. A lighter taped to his palm.

Behind him came a bunch of security guards and a couple patrolmen besides, guns drawn. Later I found out he'd taken some tourists hostage just to get up the elevator without the guards stopping it between floors. He looked at everyone, cool and casual as a polyester pimp, and gave me a nod, the baseball cap, lowercase *i* this time, low over his eyes. I moved toward him but he held up the hand with the lighter, and I decided to wait for a better opportunity.

But he had it all thought out. Loops of cord and hooks strapped on his legs. He took one and tossed it up to a railing three flights up and was climbing the wall. The cops were talking about taking him out. I flashed my badge and they lowered their guns.

I climbed the rope after him. If I hadn't been drunk I really don't know if I would have done it. And even drunk as I was, if it occurred to me we'd be climbing all the way to the damn top, three hundred feet above the observation deck at least, no way I would've done it. But I never imagined it. Every step of the way, I thought to myself, that's it, there's no way to get any higher, he'll have to stop and etcetera, but every time he found another ladder, another foothold, threw another grappling hook, and we went like that, up the stone flank of the shaft, swinging out over death, climbing ropes hanging from floodlight brackets, over slippery steel bands, up over the baffle grating and then a slope like the nose of a rocket, and that was just half the climb because then it was the radio tower, this thing of crossed beams and spines like some fossil of the king of all dinosaurs. And he kept on going like some mountain goat, and I kept going too, cutting my hands on cold bars, less and less of them and more and more darkness, and the wind trying to rip me loose. Almost did. Yanked my feet out from under me and I was hanging there dangling like a noodle from a fork, with the city slipping around under me like a big, slobbering set of jaws. I was shouting at him the whole time, mostly just to hear my own voice, saying I'd throw his ass in jail, I'd throw the fuckin' book at him and I'd throw away the goddamn key, and he was shouting too, telling me to give up, go back. But I wasn't going back and he knew it.

He stopped at a grated landing where the antenna thinned down to no wider than a man. He helped me up and we backed against the pole, arms linked behind us, panting, scared as hell, trembling, shivering. How high up we were. It was unbelievable. I didn't want to look, but I couldn't help looking, all the lights of the city spread out under us, lights in every direction all the way to the horizon and beyond, and the sky blank above us. Like we'd climbed all the way up into space, up so high that all the stars were below us now.

Slowly, together, we slid down until we were sitting on the grate. Howard held my hand real tight.

He said Hey Gus, how do you feel?

What a question! I laughed out loud.

And then I realized, I felt great. I'd never felt so great. And I told him. And I shouted it out to the whole city, how fuckin' great it all was. When I was finished shouting, it was quiet, the city, like it was watching and listening with all those millions of windows and antennas. Looked almost sensible then, like it really wasn't all some gigantic mistake.

Howard said he felt the same. He also felt like a drink. I passed him my bottle.

I said Howard, it's not gonna look like an *i*, you know.

He said

I'll curl up real tight into a ball. I'll be the dot. The lighted tower will be the stem.

I don't know, I said, I can't picture it.

He told me I was too picky, that it'd be close enough.

I told him he was under arrest.

He looked at his watch. Then held something up. He said You know what this is?

I said, A key.

He flicked it over the edge, and said

Know what I just did?

I said

You threw away the key.

He nodded, and winked at me. Then he was climbing up the antenna. I tried to get up. He'd handcuffed my wrist to the grate. That bastard.

People come up to me all the time now and ask me about him. They want to know what could've he been like, this guy inside. They come hungry for any stories I can give them, starving for stories, gulping down every word like baby birds at a worm convention. At first I wanted to take these people by the shoulders, shake them hard, tell them Stop dreaming, wake up, the guy burned himself alive and he's dead and lost and he wasn't the first and he won't be the last. But when I look at them looking to me with so much wonder, looking at *me* this way just because I was his brother and I was a part of this incredible story, I end up talking to them, sometimes for hours, and I end up telling them what a great guy Howard was. Yeah, he really was, he was an incredible guy.

One thing I was right about though. Didn't look like any *i* I ever seen.

A MILLION YEARS
FROM NOW

Whores under the streetlight all night long, lit up like vending machines. Clip-clopping in their heels, clasping themselves in the cold, steam coming out of their painted mouths. They haven't missed a night all winter.

—*It's the Junk Man*, one of them says. They crowd around.

—*What's that you got tonight, Junk Man?*

—*Piece of a airplane?*

—*Piece of a car?*

—*Where's the rest, Junk Man? Whole car, maybe, but that piece won't buy a date for you.*

—Stand aside, I say. Jezebels. Succubi.

—*Suck-a-who?*

—*Let Junk Man go. Go date his propeller.*

—*Spin it nice and good now. Junk Man.*

They part. I lock the door behind me and climb the stairs. I put down my radiator fan and go to the window. They call me the Junk Man, but it is they who are the junk, filling their veins with it night and day.

—*Hey, I see you up there*, one of them shrieks, *I see you I see you. No free shows.*

—Dirty old man.

Banshees. I let down the window cloth. They call me dirty, they who have more diseases than doctors can name.

I turn on the lamps and go to work. I add crushed glass from a cloudy pipe and a dozen brown vials, because it makes me think of her eyes, full of mist and mystery. I add eighty-eight rubber bands cut and melted back together into mobius strips, because her smile is wistful and distant, with a twist at the corner. And a broad sheet of black, sparkling sandpaper, rolled into a cone, for her voice, mirthful spikes on an earnest sea.

On my rounds, I see women. Business women, store women, college women, house women. Some of them stare back. Some look away. In each of them I look for the fragments of Paradise scattered in her race. In one, a graceful walk, but the ankles are too big. In another an elegant neck, a collar bone, but an ugly mug. Another, a modest smile, but elephant ears. Maybe if I had a million of these city women I could remake out of them one that came anywhere close to the form they deserve. Maybe a million years ago there was a woman I could love, and what I see are her traces in the endless traffic of women in the streets. Maybe a million years from now she would be bred, the pieces finally falling into place. Too long ago, too late.

Sometimes I see women stop to look through the fence at my garden on the corner, and sometimes their eyes get light and liquid for a second, before the city air congeals them once more. Sometimes I'm tempted to go up and tell them about it. There was a time when I talked. Reporters came with questions, and I talked and talked. I am the man who did the traffic posts up in bottlecaps and bits of colored glass. I am the one who welded the cars together. The one who did the thousand plastic milk jugs wired to the brick wall. And the garden. A tree of metal struts and papier-mâché. Bushes of trash cans and Styrofoam. Flowers of hangers and hubcaps, lead pipes and lamp shades, picture tubes and table fans. They asked me what it stood for, and I told them. Paradise. Since the real one is long gone. Until the real one comes again. The longest Since, the most forlorn Until that have ever been said. They stopped coming around. I stopped talking.

My fingers are stiff from cold around the handlebars, but it's been a good day. In my Key Food cart I've got a circuit board, the face of a clock, a fleckstoned flower pot, strips of chartreuse vinyl and a roll of blue party streamer. Rounding the corner I see two men at my door. One's got a shirt and a tie under his winter coat. The other's got tools and is violating my lock.

He calls himself the owner. I've been here for years, never heard from any owner. I fixed the boiler. I did the new stairs from scrapwood. I did the wires from the streetlamp to my window. He follows me upstairs, looking around. He says these places are worth something now, worth fixing. He is going to break the building into little apartments. He throws out a flat hand, like karate chops, pointing where the walls will be. He chops toward the back, and then along the floor between him and me, and then toward the front windows. He is pointing at my girl. He gets quiet. I turn on the lamps so he can see better.

—You're an artist, he says.

This is my home, I say. My voice cracks. He talks to the other man and then says I can stay for a while, if I keep out of their way. He says I can have an apartment here if I can afford the rent. I think about my veteran checks. I don't know who could afford the rent.

They leave. At last. I add a tattered umbrella, for her awkward grace. I add a garland of twine and frayed newsprint, for the way on an overcast day her face makes the clouds whirl end over end. I add an overexposed Polaroid in a glass frame, for the way on a clear day her hair makes a miracle of the sun.

I am crying like a goddamn fool, she's so goddamn beautiful.

I spend all my days with her. Nothing else is worth a fig. I add the wheels from my shopping cart, for the way she floats across the ground. The place is more cluttered now because I had to clear out the second floor. They're banging away down there now. I almost ask them for help, but the thought of their rude hands changes my mind. I do it myself. I put one knee down on the mattress for leverage and wedge my arm under her and lift her. The pain flares in my back, but she's up. I wheel her to the window and open it. The weather is better today. Spring, and the murky ice is melting in the gutters. I thread the rope through the block and tackle, secure it, and hoist her out. The pulleys are rusty but they do the job and it's not too hard to lower her to the sidewalk. By the time I get downstairs, a crowd has formed. Children gape. Men crane their necks. Women stare, with jealousy of course, but with pure awe too, they have never imagined such perfection could exist on earth. I wince at the squalor of the dirty faces and run-down buildings she has to see, the exhaust she must breathe, the blaring drumbeats from passing cars that assault her ears. I want to show her beautiful things, so she will know how beautiful she is herself. I wish I could take her to the museum so she could see it isn't all bad. A world that still has museums still has something. Instead, I guide her next door to my garden. I unlock the padlock, open the gate and wheel her over the threshold, and we stand in silence and gaze at our perfect world.

Getting her back up is more difficult, and to my shame, I injure her, letting her scrape against the face of the building. But it's nothing I can't make right. She doesn't complain. I am humbled. I add a clock face without arms, for the faith she has in me. I add a helium balloon on a white thread, for the part of her I cannot reach. I add a hundred feet of white gauze, for all the things about her I will never understand.

The sun is hard. It glares and the pavement cuts my eyes. People are everywhere. Armpits, legs, shoulders, sweaty necks, sweaty mouths, sweaty eyes. They stare at my shopping cart. It is full today, not with junk, but with white boxes, tied with pink and red ribbons. I went to half the department stores in midtown to find the things she would like. The salesgirls ran to fetch the things I wanted. After I showed them the cash. All the money I'd stowed away over the years. It was crazy to spend the money but I don't care.

I want to give her the things she deserves. I bought white dresses, a long flowing one, a strapless one, a backless one. I bought silk stockings, a lace shawl, a ruffled dressing gown. A blouse. A trumpet skirt. Satin pumps, white, with ribbon ties. Perfume, choosing from spots they sprayed along the inside of my arm. I bought a white purse, a white gold necklace and earrings, nothing too flashy, nothing the whores would wear. White, like an angel would wear. I would have bought her more casual clothes too, but she prefers to wear mine. It makes me smile, the way she rolls the waist and cuffs of my pants so they'll fit her, the way she doesn't roll the sleeves of my old shirts so that her arms flop around like a ragamuffin's. I will rearrange the closet and the dresser. Her things will get the left half of the rack, the top three drawers.

I get back to my block. All my belongings are piled on the sidewalk. Clothing, tools, sculptures, supplies. Sweaty children are picking through the piles. A little girl is opening all the umbrellas in my collection. A boy tears open a garbage bag and watches as my Styrofoam peanuts spill onto the ground. Two other boys have found my box of television antennae and are fencing on the stoop.

But she is nowhere in sight. I abandon my shopping cart and run up the stoop. The boys lash my back with the antennae. I run up the stairs, tripping once and injuring my knee. I get to the top floor. It is like the other floors now, empty. Two men sit against the bare wall, smoking. Another two men have their hands on my girl. They see me. One of them smiles, but it is a nervous smile. I take a step toward them. They take a step back.

She is unharmed. I have arrived in time.

When we are safe in my garden, I lie her down on my mattress. A spring snaps loose, bicycle spokes bend in the back, and I make everything right again. I add the delicate, curving bones of a fish, for the way she trembles in bed. I add a window screen, for the way she looks when she thinks I'm not looking. I add dozens of small round magnets, for all the things we have in common.

There is a hole inside me and it hurts because there is no food. All that is left of me is the hole where food should be, a hole where time is falling through in days and weeks.

I am not hallucinating. Amidst the brown leaves on the sidewalk is a crisp twenty dollar bill, folded, one edge fluttering in the breeze. I lunge for it and it whisks away. I dive and it darts out from under me and my elbows hit the sidewalk hard. I hear laughing, and see a group of firemen standing in the door of their firehouse. One of them waves the bill. They have it taped to a long thread. I get up. Another one tosses me a coin. I let it hit my chest and fall to the ground.

I return to my garden on the corner. I look around and there is nothing but junk. I pick up a rod and bring it down on soda bottle flowers, chicken wire bushes, plasterboard boughs. I smash a path toward the mattress on which lies a monstrosity of junk, tucked into a blanket. I lift the rod over my head.

I have frightened her. I drop the rod and sink to my knees. For the thousandth time, I apologize for my short-comings. I will never be worthy of her, but I will try very, very hard and pray that trying counts for something.

When night comes, I work by the light of the streetlamp, as the whores stand watching behind the fence. I add the upper half of a xylophone.

—*What's that for, Junk Man?*

—It is for the harmonious patterns of her thought, I explain.

I add a green circuit board melted into a minaret.

—*And what's that for, Junk Man?*

—It is for the byzantine mysteries of her dreams.

I stand back, and behold what I have wrought. I add a single pearl, genuine, in a pouch of red velvet.

—*Is that a pearl you put in there?*

—*Ooh, what's the pearl for?*

I tell them, for her soul, in which she believes, though she is too shy to admit it.

She is with me and I am in Paradise. It is winter out there but it is summer in here. I bend aside a palm frond and we watch through the fence as they stand, the fallen ones, in the harsh cold. Last night was the fiercest snowstorm I've ever seen. It got so cold the whores froze, standing on the corner. This morning they remain, in their high heels and short skirts and face paint, encased in ice and powdered with snow. They look beautiful now.

Trucks are plowing the Avenue, on which the snow is as pure as the wings of angels. The cars are fluffed in white pillows, the sidewalks are blanketed with down, the windows are sheeted in ice, and the whole city is buried in a dream.

We hear the howl of an approaching siren, and it frightens her. I tell her not to worry. It is the museum van, coming for the whores. The workers will lay them stiffly down onto boards and slide them into the backs of their van. In the museum the whores will be displayed, relics of a darker age.

The men lean over me, steam coming out of their mouths instead of words. She bends over and kisses my lips, and then the men put a mask over my nose and mouth. She gets up and walks between the flowerbeds, haloed in sunlight. Beneath the tree she turns and smiles and my chest aches with love. She is the most graceful creature in all creation. She is made of everything good about the world. She is a woman. There is nothing left to add.

WAXMAN'S SUN

Ms. Morderstern drew a dick and a pussy on the blackboard. In the back of the room, Danny Waxman humped his desk, and Danny Padro hid a smile in his hand. As she talked, Morderstern traced with her finger a path up through the pussy into the place where the cum met the egg. Then she drew sperms, taps and squiggles of chalk, and the egg was a big balloon about to get popped; and while her back was turned, Danny Waxman unzipped his fly and stuck his fingers in, looking slyly around the room. His face had a thousand freckles, a broken-looking nose, reddish-blond hair and a thin, yellow-toothed smile. Next to him, Danny Padro started to do the same thing, his mouth a big O that changed to a Q when he slid out his skinny tongue and made it waggle. Morderstern was writing words on the board: Condom. Diaphragm. "The Pill." All the kids were rocking in their seats, fighting to hold the laughs in their mouths, but when Danny Waxman lay down on the floor, stuck his legs up and pretended to be Morderstern getting herself off, air escaped loudly from Padro's lips and then everyone was laughing and Morderstern spun around.

"You think this is funny?" she said. "Wait'll you're all mommies and daddies before you turn fourteen. Then I'll be the one laughing." Ms. Morderstern wore tight pants and tight shirts which showed the shape of her body. She had short legs, big breasts, dark eyes and a pockmarked face. The class grew silent, waiting to see if she'd realize Danny Waxman was lying on the floor behind the back row.

"Danny Waxman," she said. "Danny Waxman."

Danny climbed back into his chair.

"Danny Waxman. Stand up," she said, a hand on her hip and a mean wrinkle on her lip, "...and tell the class about your father."

Everyone was looking at him, except for Padro, who didn't look up from his desk. Danny Waxman stood up. There were giggles. His face felt prickling hot.

"What's the matter?" Morderstern said, "Okay I'll give you a hint. Your father probably couldn't keep his fly closed either."

"Man o man!" whispered Padro, glancing up fearfully, his mouth now a little o. "She doggin' you."

Danny Waxman looked over at the gray window. He zipped his fly.

"What are you smiling at Danny? Something funny about your father? Why don't you tell us?"

The smile was something glued to his face. Padro looked up at him, his big round eyes saying: Go on, tell her. Waxman looked down at his sneakers.

"What's the matter?" Morderstern said. "You must know *something* about him.... Okay I'll give you a hint. He drives a subway train. You want another hint? He's an alcoholic. Now go on, tell us some more."

Danny didn't move. Outside, the clouds broke and through the criss-crossed window bars sunlight grilled the classroom.

"Oh, that's right," Morderstern said. "You don't *know* anything else about your father." She was shouting now. "You'd better quit horsing around and pay attention here, or else you'll make the same mistake your father made and have a kid you don't want with a woman you don't want and *your* kid will grow up like a wild hooligan too!"

There was a tremor at the corner of Waxman's smile. In the second row, Adriel, a girl with pink-framed glasses and a square jaw stood up. She was usually quiet and got good grades, but now she screamed, "You can't say that to him. It doesn't matter *who* his dad is. You're a bad teacher!"

Danny Padro stood up. Like Adriel, his eyes were shiny with tears. "Yeah. You shouldna said that. Danny's no mistake. You the mistake. You so ugly yo mamma was a test tube and yo papa was a dirty rubber from the gutter."

And then Saed, the fat Arab kid in row six seat five piped in with his high scratchy voice, "Yeah and den you was born outa asshola elephant inda zoo—" He squatted over his chair and made an asshole noise and the whole class blew up with jeers and shouting. Morderstern picked up her canvas bag and walked out of the room, seconds before the bell.

Danny and Danny walked eyeing the sidewalk, sparkling and cracked in the sun. They kept both of their bikes at Danny Waxman's place, because if you rode in Danny Padro's neighborhood your bike might get taken from you. Danny and Mrs. Waxman lived in Brooklyn Heights, a neighborhood with cops and stores, private schools covered with vines and seven different subways in one stop. But the home itself was small and dark, a basement apartment with little barred windows in the front and back bedrooms, and no light at all in the living room and the cave where the kitchen was. They had to tiptoe past Mrs. Waxman's room; she slept all day because she worked the night shift in a subway token booth. Danny Padro checked the refrigerator like he always did, but as usual there was nothing to eat, just a carton of eggs and then Miracle Whip and ketchup in the door shelf.

They carried their bikes up the steps onto the sidewalk. Waxman rode like a maniac, and Padro had trouble keeping up. They weaved through traffic, churning up a cloud of honks, screeching brakes, shouts and shaking fists. They wheelied through crowds along the Promenade, the walk-way over the Brooklyn–Queens Expressway where you could see Manhattan sparkle terrifically across the river, towers tall as the sky, more buildings than you could visit in a lifetime. They rode down Suicide Hill, the steepest street on earth, trying not to swerve or brake, and Waxman went down faster and faster every time, smiling his thin smile, eyes tearing from the speed.

When the sun began to sink over New Jersey and the sky closed in, dyeing houses purple and streets dark blue, they left their bikes at Waxman's place and went to Padro's down past the F and G train stop. Danny Padro and his mom lived in the Gawanas projects, in one of a dozen brown giants that loomed moodily over the streets. But inside, the apartment was nice, with plants and decorations and bead curtains instead of doors, and his mom liked to cook so there was always food. And even though Danny Padro's father had a new wife and other kids and an important job as a captain in the Transit Police, some nights he still came over and joked around with them, telling stories and wrestling them on the rug. But that night Mr. Padro didn't come.

Restless after dinner, they ran up ten flights of stairs and tumbled out onto the roof. Around them, Brooklyn by night spun out in a million droplets of light. They walked around to the side that faced Manhattan. They leaned forward and rested their arms on the low wall, still panting from the stairs. After a silent minute, Padro spoke.

"You a bullshitter," he said.

They weren't looking at each other, just straight ahead at the skyline.

"No I'm not."

"You told me your dad was a nuclear engineer."

"He *was* one, back in Russia." Waxman said. "'Sides, he's not just a motorman."

"How do you know what he is? You don't even know him."

"I do know him."

Danny Padro thought for a moment. "You a bullshitter," he said.

"No I'm not."

"Well what is he then?"

When Danny Waxman pointed, their heads tilted together and they both sighted along his outstretched arm to where Manhattan stood up to the night with an alien wonder. "New York City," he said, "is the brightest thing in the whole world. It's so bright you can see it all the way from the moon. It's brighter than anything in the whole entire solar system. 'Xcept for the sun."

"...'xcept for the sun," Padro echoed.

"The sun is a gigantic ball of nuclear fire, as big as a million Earths. It radiates heat and light so we can live and see. So when the scientists wanted to light New York at night, they sent my father to go get a piece of sun."

Over the tops of the tallest buildings, red lights winked hypnotically, warding planes away.

"And he went there, and he got a piece. And every night, my father drives it around underneath the city, and wherever my father goes the buildings above him soak up heat and light and power to make things run. Without my dad, the city would be dark and blind, and the city's sun would melt down, and you, and me, and Morder-bitch, and everybody in Brooklyn and Manhattan and the whole city would get cold and sick and blind and get hair falling out and six fingers and toes and die."

Danny walked home by himself. His mother was gone to work, but still he tiptoed through the dark rooms. In his bedroom, a little light from the other apartments across the backyards gave a pale outline to the crumpled clothes, comic books, baseball cards and pizzeria paper bags scattered on the floor. Leaning against the wall were the dismantled metal pieces of his bed frame. The mattress rested at an angle just inside the door so that only someone his size could enter. He got into bed and turned on the small black and white TV on the floor next to him — no sound, just the gray washed-out light of the picture. In bed, floating in the eerie light, he imagined his father's return to Earth with the captured piece of sun in tow. He saw the needle-thin craft piercing the atmosphere of the big blue planet, shooting down in a long arc through the sky, the ball of fire blazing and streaming, like a shooting star — it must have been like that, like a shooting star. Danny had never seen a shooting star, and he knew why too, because a shooting star is not as bright as a New York night. As he drifted off to sleep, he felt the floor rumble. When the subway passed beneath him, the TV picture grew sharper and brighter, lighting up the room like a full moon, and then subsided, and Danny sighed and was asleep.

The next day in school, the other kids treated Danny differently. They felt sorry for him. He could see it in their averted eyes. The proof came at lunch hour when he badmouthed Saed's mother and Saed didn't badmouth his mother back. It was worse than the worst insult. And Padro was the guiltiest of all, with his big moony eyes all scared somebody would say something about yesterday. Back in class after lunch, Waxman horsed around more than ever. Nobody laughed or paid any attention to him, not even Ms. Morderstern, but he did it anyway, to show he wasn't beaten.

When he came home from school, he found his mom asleep on the couch. Sometimes she did that, so tired she couldn't even make it to her room. Her breaths were heavy and slow; her arms were folded in front of her chest and her hip rose up like a steep hill. She was still dressed. Her face was ashy and half-crushed by the cushion; her hair was long and frazzled, with some gray ones. She would run her fingers through it sometimes, in front of the mirror; she would say *I've let myself go*, and Danny would think of the time she cut herself trying to catch a falling knife — her face melted and hardened, and laughed and cried at the same time, and he saw she looked old.

"Mom," Danny whispered, sitting forward on the foot-rest of the recliner.

"Hmm?" Her eyes were still closed.

"You should go to bed. Your neck gets hurt when you sleep on the couch."

"Mmm-hmmn."

"I'm going to see my Dad."

Her eyes opened, and then fell closed again. "You can't Danny."

"I can."

"You don't know where to find him."

"Yeah I do. I got a subway map. I know how to get there. I'll be careful, I promise."

"We've talked about it before Danny."

75

"He is my father, isn't he?"

"Of course he is sweetheart."

"Then can I go see him?"

"We'll talk in the morning, after work," she mumbled.

Danny waited a couple seconds, and said in a lower voice, "then can I go see him tonight, Mom?"

"Okay we'll talk in the morning." The last words were barely even a whisper

"Okay. Thanks, Mom."

"Hmm."

He opened his closet door and felt around on the top shelf until he found his flashlight. He swept the coats down the rack, revealing the back wall. Taped up to it was a picture from a magazine of a woman wearing an open leather jacket and boots and nothing else leaning against the side of a helicopter. Next to that was a subway map, with the train lines in different colors. He kissed the woman, then peeled the map off the wall and folded it carefully. He picked up his Mets jacket from the floor and his sneakers, and tiptoed out through the living room, past his sleeping mother and out the door.

When the train came, he got in the last car and watched the station fall away and the occasional lights of the tunnel rustling off like sparks from a blaze. When he saw water spattering from leaks in the ceiling, he knew the East River was above. His eyes skimmed the yellow rail that ran along the tunnel wall, seamlessly, the top half caked with soot; he thought of all the miles and miles of this sooty yellow rail.

In Manhattan, the train started to fill up. At Wall Street the dark suits bustled in and stood stiffly around the poles. A little further up Chinese people with shrunken faces and plain canvas shoes got on, slumped into the seats, and got off a couple stops later. At thirty fourth and forty second the train got packed full of all kinds: African ladies with copper-dyed hair, full of beads and braided up into giant cones; tiny Indian ladies with the third eye on their foreheads; huge Italian men that took up two seats, faces melting like mozzarella over their chests. For three stops the most beautiful girl he'd ever seen sat across from him, mouthing with her full lips the words from a tiny Jewish Bible, turning the pages, backwards, never looking up.

At Eighty Sixth Street, all the white people who were good-looking or dressed nice got off. As the numbers of the streets climbed into the hundreds the train emptied out. Some Puerto Rican kids were staring at him for a while, trying to get him to look back so they could pick a fight, but then they got off too. After Harlem, there were just some old people, speaking quietly in rough-sounding languages. Danny went to the front of the car, slid open the door and rode on the outside, in the roar and shudder of the train and the tunnel. He put one foot on the rounded ledge of each car, holding the handles of both doors, balancing as his legs were forced open and closed over the dark crevice. Out of nervousness, he smiled, and in a minute everything was fine. He made believe that the cars had come apart, and his mother was trapped in one and his father was trapped in the other, and he alone was holding the two cars together.

After a long series of gloomily fluorescent stations, the train pulled into 241st Street and the last stop announcement barked from the speakers. Danny got off the train and hid behind a staircase as the conductor walked through the cars checking for people. When the search was done, Danny scrambled back over the chains into the space between cars.

The train jerked and lumbered slowly into the tunnel. Before long, he saw other tracks through arches in the dusky wall. The arches turned into pillars and he spotted another train moving in parallel four or five tracks down. Tracks came to an end or split off into other tracks that ended; on them, trains hibernated, still and dark. His own train veered onto a side track, slowing to a creep and finally stopping with a crude hiss from below. He clambered down onto the track, keeping his flashlight to the uneven tunnel floor, illuminating dirt and dark puddles and every so often a rat's tail swishing out of the spume of light. Only the tracks looked clean—straight and sharp, like endless knives.

The tunnels ended in a wide, well-lit cavern with tile walls and a vaulted ceiling. There were no platforms, just twenty or so parallel tracks, running the length of the floor. Standing on the tracks were subway cars of all kinds, the old 6 trains with rounded black roofs and sides painted red, the heavyset B and D trains with grooved flanks and gray seats, the Japanese F trains with orange and yellow seats facing in all directions, and the newer Japanese 4s and 5s with LCD signs and seats in long benches against either wall. And there as well were the elusive yellow service engines — more like outdoor train engines than subway cars—with raised cabins, long, boxy snouts, and one bright headlight in the middle.

Danny walked alongside a parked train, studying the wheels. He heard a shout and jumped. A few tracks down, a motorman was waving and hollering from the window of his cabin. The last car of his train had come unlatched and was starting to roll toward two workers kneeling and hammering on a bent track. A big man came running from around the car, leapt into the path, threw his hands up against the edge of the car and set his weight against it. The car was forcing him back, first one quick step and then another. The muscles of his arms stood out bright red against his blue cut-off work shirt. The car pushed him back more, but the steps were shorter and further between, and then he took his stand, leaning his thick shoulders all the way into it, his head beneath the flooring ledge.

The car stopped. The track workers cheered, and came over lugging iron vises which they tightened with wrenches onto the tracks. The man stepped out from under the massive car and it rolled up against the grips. He showed his teeth, more of a grimace than a smile, rubbing the back of his neck, and then he saw Danny.

The grimace froze on his broad red face. For a moment Danny feared the man might eat him.

"Are you my father?" Danny said, in the deepest voice he could manage.

The man continued to smile while sweat ran down the side of his face. There was a flat bottle in his pants pocket; Danny could see the clear glass neck and red plastic cap jutting out at an angle.

"Danny," he said. His voice was rough, as though from disuse. He had a thick accent. "What you do here, eh?"

"You're not my father," Danny said, swallowing a lump of fear.

"What the hell you talking 'bout?" he growled. He walked over to Danny, grabbed him by the upper arms and lifted him in the air. "You think I don't know my own kid?"

Danny looked down between the man's muscular arms to his huge flushed face. Even his eyes were red.

"You're a bullshitter," Danny said. "You say you're my father but you never did crap for me. You never came around and you hate me and Mom. You're not my father. You're just a bullshitter."

"You think I owe something to you?" his father said, a violent tremor in his voice.

Danny said nothing.

"You think I owe something? What do I owe to you?"

"Big bullshitter," Danny said. It was a brave thing to say. He wanted to show how brave he was, but he couldn't keep the tears out of his eyes, and his voice sounded as hoarse as Saed's.

"All right." Mr. Waxman put Danny back on the ground. "You want I do something for you, fine, you got it. Anything you want."

"You swear?"

"Yes. What the fuck. I swear." There were tears in Mr. Waxman's eyes too. He turned his head toward the ceiling and Danny watched the movements of his thick-veined neck as he spoke in an overloud voice, slurring his words. "Waxman may be fuck-up. But Waxman never go back on word. At least I can teach to you that. So OK I have sweared. Now what it is you want? You want for me come visit? Bring to your mother flowers? Take you to baseball game? You name it I do it."

"I want to drive your train."

"No."

"You swore!" Danny said.

Mr. Waxman towered over him, his face like a furnace.

"You're a bullshitter," Danny said.

Mr. Waxman's arms tensed. He grew so hot it seemed his hair would catch fire and molten lava would erupt from his eyes. Then, he turned his back to Danny. He unscrewed the cap from his bottle and took a long pull, screwed the cap back on and returned the bottle to his pocket. He wheeled back around too fast and almost fell, tossing up his hands at first for balance and then in despair.

"All right. Fine! Damned machine just 'bout runs self anyway. No steering wheel. No clutch. Just accelerator. I always say kid could do it. You go 'head. See how hot is it.

See what kind of life has your bullshit father. You go ride train. I stay here. Drink all night."

They walked across track after track, hopping over the rails. The final track was set apart from the rest. Backed against the wall was a service engine, like the others but larger, and not yellow but bright gold. It was ferocious-looking, with a long snout in front of a jutting cabin and burnished wheels like circular blades. From the back of the engine, a chain as thick as Danny was laid out along a groove between the tracks, disappearing under a huge round door like the vault of a safe. His father lifted him into the cabin. "Danny. Simple rule. Keep lever right in middle. No faster than middle. Once you get to middle, don't speed up no more or else everything get too hot. Whatever you do, don't switch tracks, don't go elevated tracks. If sun gets outside, whole city burns."

Danny shut the door and waved through the window. A siren wailed and red lights whirred all across the ceiling of the cavern. Everywhere, blue-shirted workers ran for cover. His father backed off to the nearest fire wall. His face slowly lost its anger, the bushy eyebrows lifting, the jaw loosening. But then the features kept on going, becoming an expression of terror. Only now, it seemed, he had fully realized what he had done. He was holding out his palms, waving his arms, shaking his head.

Too late. The traffic light against the tile cavern wall has turned green and Danny has slid the accelerator forward. In the shaded side-view mirror he sees the rising chain and the opening vault and an impossible brightness. The chain tautens and the giant white-hot globe is dragged from the vault. Immediately, the walls of the cabin are too hot to touch. Danny slumps down in the seat but in a second the vinyl is so hot it scalds his back. He stands, takes off his jacket and wraps it around the handle of the accelerator, inching it forward, hoping to gain more distance from the burning scoop of sun rolling in its harness behind him.

His own single headlight is hardly needed; the sunlight jostles through the gaps between train and wall, and the tunnel is lit in strobing daylight. The glare from the puddles and silver tracks ahead makes him wince. It is too hot; he imagines he's letting the sun get too close, and presses the accelerator forward. In the bath of heat he feels a brief coolness against his leg. He has wet his pants. There are no stations along this tunnel and thus he has no idea how fast he is going or what is overhead. He just wants the ride to be over. He presses the accelerator forward, just a quarter of an inch more. He tries to think of school tomorrow, and their faces when he tells them all. They won't believe him, so then he'll open his lunchbox and show them a glowing seed-sized nugget of sun he's taken as a trophy and then they'll believe, all of them except for Morderstern, and she'll make another crack about his dad, but his dad has come to live with them now and he comes to school and walks into the classroom and Morderstern! Morderstern will eat her words when he towers over her with his big arms folded, and she will on her knees she will beg forgiveness, please Mr. Waxman please I'm sorry I didn't mean it honest.

The sun subway is lighting up the tunnel like a flash fire in a drought. It is going faster than specifications allow, faster than thought possible. It is racing south, leaving the Bronx behind, and overhead, Harlem is in chaos. Every light in every building goes on, pouring harsh illumination into the streets, and the charge builds and overloads and every bulb bursts in every socket, and there is a blackout, and rampaging mobs loot the stores, smashing the windows and grabbing all the things they've seen but could never touch. They roll shopping carts full of fine things down the streets, drawing on the power crackling in the hot pavement under their feet, and shop owners stand by, faces in hands.

And the engine plummets on, headlong down the baking tunnel. Danny wipes his ruddy hair from his eyes, sees his hand on the accelerator, and trembles with fear. It's three-fourths of the way forward. The engine moves faster and faster, and the sun is as close as ever, maybe even closer, looming and rolling and burning: the heat is thick as blood. He tries to ease back on the lever, but he hears hissing behind him and the mirror is nothing but sun. "Stop it!" he screams over his shoulder. "Cut it out, will you?" But the wild sun won't let up, and in terror he presses the lever as far forward as it will go. Ahead, the track splits, curving off and going straight ahead. It comes up fast, and when he feels the wrenching jolt from below, he knows the engine was supposed to turn but instead it jumped the tracks and is going straight ahead down a new tunnel, and behind him the sun is out of control, rolling left and right and smashing first one wall and then the other, ripping the life out of the tunnel behind him with its tremendous density.

And now the train is on an express track and gaining speed by the second. He barrels through a station, and soon after, another. The stations provide a rhythm with noisy echoes, punctuating the muffled clatter of the tunnels like cymbal crashes. Above, Uptown is in turmoil. Red, roiling heat explodes from the grates, searing the well-kept sidewalks. Soles of topsiders melt away, and with scorched feet pedestrians run to their high-rises, and the elevators rise like mercury in a thermometer, and the heat follows them all the way up to the penthouses — they can't escape it — they are transfixed by their own supercharged halogen lights, and even their shadows burn.

Next the empty office buildings of Midtown light up like ghosts of themselves, phones ringing, monitors glowing, copiers copying, faxes faxing back and forth, the hundreds of thousands of glass windows consumed with brightness, mirroring each other in an endless, uncontrollable reflex until all of Manhattan gleams fiercely gold, like a sun in a diamond. And all the people of the outer boroughs wake and rise to see it. They watch from the rooftops of Starrett City, Gravesend, Crown Heights, Flatbush, Fox Hills, Red Hook, Brownsville, Whitestone, Bensonhurst, Ozone Park, Rego Park, Jackson Heights, Jamaica, Astoria, New Brighton, Sunnyside, Flushing, and Corona, all of them warmed by the glow, marveling together at their city, as though they have just now arrived.

In the Grand Street station, Mrs. Waxman is perched on her tall chair, fanning herself with a magazine. It is stuffy and still; there is no sound other than a constant, resonating hum which slips into the bottom of the ears, and down beneath the floor, and seems to lift the steel-armored booth a fraction of an inch from the ground. She is staring off through the bulletproof glass, letting her thoughts wander through the far tunnels of her mind; her thoughts wander all night, every night, nothing to rein them in. Facing her on the wall of the opposite platform is a picture of a black man and a black woman, in tuxedo and evening gown, standing on a penthouse balcony while far below New York blushes deep red with sunset. They look into each other's eyes. A bottle and two glasses of scotch stand on the table in the lower corner of the frame, and the final light from the sun makes the scotch blaze like gold. In a few moments the black man and the black woman will put their arms lightly around each other. They will sway slowly, dancing to the sound of the city, a sound like soft music from this giddy height. They will dance and hold each other closer, bodies as big as the city below, grateful to life for the tuxedo and evening gown, sunset and scotch and balcony and city and one another. It is like a dream, the man and woman will think, it is like an advertisement they had seen in the subway stations when times were more difficult, and they will smile at this. And then their soft, dark lips will touch. Mrs. Waxman feels the kiss; it is always the same kiss she feels, his kiss, when they made love, his body tremendous and hot and opening within her, and through his kiss his tongue would find its way, a root seeking soil, and it was almost too much for her, but she liked the idea that he needed to be inside her two ways and not just one, and she liked to think too that it was this that allowed Danny to begin to flower.

Danny's skin is baked bright red, and the tears turn to steam as they roll down his face. The heat in the tracks has melted the switching systems, and he is speeding down a line that was not meant for him. The tunnel is clattering by and the sun is dawning behind him and there is nothing he can do. If only his father was just a regular drunken motorman. If only he'd had no father. The air is so dry he can barely breathe, so hot it scalds his lungs. His engine is screaming through another station. He sees something familiar about it, something about the tiles in the walls, and then for an instant he catches sight of his mother in the token booth. He pounds on his window but then the glass of her booth fires back the blinding sun and already he is back in the tunnel. Now he knows, Grand Street, the last stop in Manhattan on the B D Q line. Ahead the tunnel ends in a hole with stars; the track will lead over the Manhattan Bridge and into Brooklyn. He can think of nothing but the cool outside air, and he presses all his weight against the accelerator. And then there is something in the track against the night, where the tunnel ends and the sky begins. It is a man standing with legs wide apart. A big man in a blue uniform, with a brown face and a black beard. Danny recognizes him. He presses the horn, loud blasts, out of the way, out of the way. Captain Padro doesn't get out of the way. He raises something in his hands, and Danny sees a star on the windshield, and the hotness is no longer outside but inside, in his chest, blazing and blossoming through his limbs. He stumbles back, off the accelerator. On his back on the cabin floor, he feels the engine slow and hears the chain rattling and the sun surging in, but he's not afraid now, because it's already with him.

As soon as she heard the rumble of the engine, it was there, roaring through the station, chain flying behind. She saw her son pounding on the window, and then came the light, an explosion undoing all of existence. She could barely cover her eyes before it was gone, leaving a trail of smoke and burning garbage in the tracks. And now she was running, her hand skimming the still-warm yellow rail, getting hotter and hotter, and when the curve in the tunnel began to straighten she felt the blast of heat and light and knew she could go no further.

After the radiation-suited workmen had packed the sun away in a flameproof crate, hauled it off and put out the track fires, Mrs. Waxman searched the smelted wreckage, but the cabin was entirely gone. Danny had merged with the sun and left none of himself behind. She looked up from the blackened tracks, and saw a figure standing in the tunnel. It was Mr. Waxman, his face red and anguished. They walked slowly toward each other, chests constricted by sobs, vision blurred by tears and soot.

Their grief was beyond what they could bear, and the radiation was not long in taking effect. Mr. Waxman felt his body tighten; his chest became hard, and flat, his arms fell to his sides and he couldn't feel his legs. His back grew hunched and a long cord grew out from behind him, snaking off into the distance. Mrs. Waxman saw his body shrinking behind him like a wedge. She reached out to touch him, and his skin was unfeeling, neither warm nor cool. But in his heart he was feeling a warm lustrous charge. He tried to tell her, but his tongue became hard and brassy, and stuck out from his face, and another prong was forming below, shining and reflecting the tunnel light. And Mrs. Waxman felt her body stiffen, her face becoming smooth like a shell. She tried to scream, but no sound emerged from her mouth which hardened and remained open, a slot, and another slot formed below.

And they came together in a final embrace, plug and socket, joined in a closed circuit, the energy churning inward, ever consuming its tail, a far more controllable way of bringing light. For when Captain Padro filed his report, it was determined the power source would be kept far from the city, to be diffused through an interminable, snarling webwork of wires — so that never again would so much power be so close by to citizens who might claim it as their natural right. And all frustration, rage, and violence would be channelled inward, just like the city's own energy, never to escape, except for sometimes, in the form of a small, unwanted spark.

MAXIMUM
CARNAGE

A sentor is a mutant of craven science. The top half of a sentor is the top half of a man. The bottom half is a motorcycle.

Right now the sentors are attacking P.S. 96 in Flushing, Queens.

The only one who can stop them is Roxor.

There is a girl named roxanne. It sounds like Rocks Anne. My name is Roxor. Roxor spelled backwards is roxoR. It is the perfect name. The x is safe in the middle.

Kenny with the big head is giving his superhero report. His superhero's name is Incman. He holds it up. He reads from the back and we look at the front.

Incman gets his powers from different kinds of incs he drinks. If he drinks disappearing inc, he disappears. If he drinks India inc he teleports to India. If he drinks indelible inc he will not bleed.

Incman is nothing compared to me.

The sentors are riding around the playground. They have beards and they shout war cries and fart black smoke. They have come to kidnap the girls. They need the girls for food. On their black leather seats, they will carry the girls back to their laboratory and pump out their girl blood. Girl blood fuels their engines. In the laboratory, the girls will be pumped. Pumped and pumped.

Roxanne

The class is looking with big eyes. roxanne takes her hand away, and it lies on the desk like a dead dog.

Roxanne, Ms. Manolo is saying with her square mouth. Can I see you outside?

They start to crackup as she walks down the aisle. The talk is in the green hallway, in front of the closed door. There are thin hair wires in the door window, and thin hair shadows on the floor squares.

Roxanne, please don't think I'm punishing you. But what you were doing is not appropriate behavior in a public place. Would you like someone to talk to about it?

roxanne shakes her head.

I think it might be a good idea. Why don't you talk to our counselor, Ms. Featherbest, okay? You like Ms. Featherbest, don't you? She's very nice.

Ms. Featherbest has very nice handwriting. Like this.

Roxanne is a very bright 10 year-old, who suffers from low self-esteem, a disturbance of the aggressive drive, and a fixation at the anal-sadistic stage.

The playground is filled with puddles of blood. I come, but not in time to save Kenny. His big head is a big flat tiretread of flesh and red hair. The sentor who ran over Kenny's head sees me and revs his engine and charges. He charges with a lance which is a pointy pole. I am not worried. When the lance hits me in the chest it doesn't even go through my skin. Nothing can go through my skin. The lance breaks in half. And the sentor says uh-oh. And I pick up the sharp half and push it into the sentor's curly chest. And it makes a squishy sound. And when I take it out again there is a red wound. And I do it again and I make a wound inside the wound.

Tony with the soft voice is in the front, doing his superhero report. His superhero's name is The King of Kings. The King of Kings comes from Kings County, which is Brooklyn. The King of Kings has all the powers of all the Kings. He has King Arthur's sword and the strength of Conan, who was a king too. The King of Kings has a crown and a big robe.

Thank you, Tony. That was very creative, Ms. Manolo says.

Once I was a little boy. Some say once I was a little girl but that's a lie. One day, I was walking out on the shore of Flushing Bay, walking out on a dock of wood, tossing pieces of rock into the scummy water, and I slipped. No, I didn't slip. It wasn't my fault. The old rotting wood broke and I fell like falling through a trap door. I dropped like an anchor no like a rock into the scummy contaminated water, where there was a sunken submarine from the Brooklyn Navy Yard that sunk when the Brooklyn Navy was on a secret mission to Queens. And it was radioactive and so the water was contaminated with radioactive contamination. And when I came up out of the glowing gooey water, I was Roxor, the most powerful superhero in Queens, and the whole city too.

Skin like armor. Skin like rock. Nothing goes through.

And now in the playground, I step over a spinning wheel and a jerking arm, and I move into the battle, and I leave footprints of sticky blood. A sentor sees me and pops a wheelie and comes at me with a trident which is like a big fork. But I don't flinch, I don't even blink, and the points of the trident break off like the points of a plastic fork. The sentor skids out and scrapes his side against the scrapey playground, ripping off pieces of skin and paint. I pick up the points of the trident, and put them into the sentor's face. I put one of the points into his forehead and it sticks there. I put the other two points into his eyeholes. The point that went into the one eyehole falls out and the eyeball is stuck to it and comes out too. The point that went into the other eyehole stays in but the eyeball gets pushed out and slides down the sentor's face, down into his beard, and it hangs there like a piece of food.

I laugh. I pull out my sausage and splash the dead sentor with piss. I piss and laugh as the piss steams off the dead ugly face.

Holy shit, his soft voice says. What do you think you're doing? You can't use that. This is the Boys room. Can't you read?

Tony stands in the doorway. He is all bright in the bright white squares.

In the playground, they ride in a circle around the group of girls, and their tires leave a rubber ring. The girls are scared. Tony runs up to hit one with his lunchbox, and a sentor takes a stiletto which is a knife that pops out and puts it into Tony's neck. Tony falls to the ground and his lunchbox falls to the ground and opens next to his head. The engines roar and the mouths shout and one of them yells Hey Roxor I heard you once were a whining little girl a slutty whining little brat of a girl and that's what you'll always be, so give up, give up and join the other girls, and I say That's a lie and your flesh will be my proving ground, your sorry mutated hide is not long for this world you mutant and your mutant ass is mine. I pull the knife out from Tony's throat and from the knifehole Tony's blood spurts into his open lunchbox and mixes with the red punch leaking out of the punchbox through a straw. I go up to the sentor and I put the knife in so deep that my hand goes all the way in.

I take out my hand and the knife has blood all over it, and I say to the sentor Look at the mess you made! That's very bad of you. Clean it up now. Lick it clean.

And the sentor opens his mouth and licks it clean.

The boys are on the one side of the playground and the girls are on the other side. The boys have their pieces of paper out and they are talking about their superheroes.

What are you looking at?

roxanne has her picture out too, but they try to grab it and so she puts it away.

Paul with the fat cheeks says go away go play with the girls.

suck my dick!

Shouldn't have said it. The boys laugh so much they never stop.

The girls see roxanne coming and whisper and move away.

roxanne goes through the gate into the kiddy park. It is full of animals. There is a horse, and a whale, and a hippopotamus, and a giraffe. They are made out of the same thing as the playground which is concrete. Yesterday, there was a little book lying on the sidewalk. It had pictures. It said once upon a time, all the animals were happy, and there was a boy and a girl, and they all lived together and played in a land with trees and grass.

Then bad things happened. But one day it will be like that again.

The monitor isn't looking and roxanne sneaks out through the hole in the fence and runs down the street. It is a windy day, and a newspaper is flying in the wind. The pictures spin and the words twist. What would it be like to be the picture? Or the twisting words?

The comic book store has millions of comics. The best one is Violator. Violator grabs the little badguy and first he takes his head and pulls it halfway off his neckbone. Then he jumps on the badguy with feet that have claws, over and over until the badguy is a shriveled up pile of skin and blood. He does it again and again until he is very tired and sweaty and drooling.

Uncle Edward has a blue anchor on his curly chest. Anchors sink but his doesn't. In the bathtub it bobs on the water.

Poor little badguy, you're no match for Roxor. You're too puny. You need protein. Sausage has lots of protein.

I stand with my hands on my hips. And the sentor opens his mouth and I smile. Everywhere in the playground there is carnage. There is blood and bodies and flames coming out of burning sentor engines. And Paul lies on the ground and his fat cheeks have been torn off and his skinny tongue is feeling around for them and he is crying. And the windy sky is red like a wound, and P.S. 96 is redder like a wound inside the wound. And there are broken windows, and there are booming noises from the guns because now the sentors have guns, and uh-oh.

That's not how you do it.

08

Let me show you.

07

The older boy presses up from behind, and his hand is reaching into his pocket and his knuckles are bony, and he puts a quarter in. There are older boys in the arcade, and there are colory lights and sounds and joysticks with knobs that look like candy. He puts his hands over roxanne's hands on the gun. The badguys pop up in windows and doorways and get blown away, and when they die they scream and blood explodes out of them, and when they die he presses his body and he is bony and she is squished up against the game.

Two of them have uzis which are little machine guns. They pull the triggers and the gunholes light up and boom. But I am not worried. I yawn and I stretch my arms. The hot bullets zing off my chest. It doesn't hurt. The bullets are like raindrops from the clouds. I walk toward them and reach out with both hands and take the guns away from the sentors. My turn, I say. I squeeze the triggers and watch the bullets go into their bellies until they are bloody messes. They try to get away, and I shoot out their back tires and they skid out, and their hearts and intestines and livers and stomachs spill out from their opened-up bellies when they scrape across the concrete.

Lunchtime is already over. Ms. Manolo is mad and she makes a mark in her book, and everybody waits for roxanne to sit down. Marcus with the sticking out teeth is holding up his picture. His superhero is Garbage Man. By day Garbage Man is a garbage man. By night he is a man made out of garbage.

He is master of the element of garbage. He can make a garbage storm. He can make a garbage avalanche. Wherever there is garbage, Garbage Man has power.

A sentor has got Ms. Manolo and he takes his sword and shoves it up her, up to the handle and Ms. Manolo moans and whines. I walk up and reach into her legs and take the sword out. And I swing the sword, and I slash red stripes into the sentor. And the boys are watching, and they cheer:

𝕱𝖎𝖓𝖎𝖘𝖍 𝕳𝖎𝖒!

and I swing the sword and cut off the sentor's head. And the head flies through the air. And the head is still alive, because cut-off heads live for ten seconds. That's what it says in Violator. So the cut-off head is still alive flying through the air, and it watches the place where it used to be, where there is a colory fountain of blood. And the cut-off head's eyes watch me as I reach my fist into the spouting neckhole and I pull out the whole spine, and I hold it up so it moves and creaks in the blowing wind. And everyone cheers. And I turn my face up to the windy sky and I laugh Ha Ha! And I grab the headless sentor by the shoulders and I hump the empty neckhole.

Thank you, Marcus, that was very inventive. Now, Roxanne, come up and tell us about your superhero. Ms. Manolo sits straight on her seat, blinking and smiling like a commercial woman. The class is looking. Whispering.

my superhero is the greatest most powerful superhero in Queens and in the whole city

Yeah right

You hush, you've had your turn. Roxanne, louder please.

my superhero

His skin can't be pierced! the Sentor shouts but then can't speak anymore. I slice him like a salami into fifteen pieces.

superhero in Queens

Another one begs for mercy but I crave maximum carnage. I cut him open and I reach in and I fold him and I turn him inside-out.

once he was a little

Whining little brat of a

into the scummy water

Wound inside the wound I make

was contaminated with

Lick it clean I laugh

and when she when he came up

His skin can't be pierced! the Sentors shout.

and his skin can't be pierced by a sword or bullets or even a chainsaw or even a chainsaw made out of kryptonite. Not by anything in the universe.

Big deal!

Roxor! What a stupid name!

Superheroes don't change from girls to boys. You gotta have a girl superhero.

Quiet, children. It's *her* hero. It can be any way she wants.

I know how to kill him!

Me too!

do not!

Children.

The bell rings.

Have a nice day. Don't run.

I know how to kill him! One of the Sentors wheels off to the kiddy playground and picks up the concrete horse and comes back with it. Take this, Roxor!

The horse comes down like a rock. I try to catch it and hold it, but I fall down on my knees because it is so heavy.

Another sentor rides off to the kiddy park and rips out the giraffe. He comes back and throws it on top of me. It is so heavy that I fall down.

Then they toss the hippopotamus on top.

Then they toss the whale. It lands with a crunch.

They are piling on, piling and piling on, shouting.

We'll show you how to deal with Roxor.

There are pieces of light and playground between their arms and legs, but there is no breathing. A bony elbow. A knee. A sneaker. Hands and knuckles. They shout and crunch. They are too heavy. And the concrete is scrapey and hard and no breathing.

We got you now. We'll give it to you good.

Get the picture.

Come on Roxor, let's see your dick, let's see it.

Where is it? The picture. Come on.

Roxor's dead. Dead. Say it. Say it. Say it like you mean it.

𝔉𝔦𝔫𝔦𝔰𝔥 𝔥𝔦𝔪!

The pile stops moving.

YOU LOSE!

They laugh so much they never stop.

Insert coin to continue.

But then they stop.

09

Something rises up out of the carnage.

08

A picture and twisting words.

07

I rise into the wind and I fly.

06

And everyone looks up.

05

I circle in the circling wind.

04

I fly high above the playground.

03

So high the cement looks smooth like the sky.

02

So high the animals look like real.

01

So high that Brooklyn and Queens are the same thing.

00

ARCADIA INC.

ON MORPHEUS, RELATING TO ORPHEUS...

Morpheus is not a famous actor. There are a few people, however, other aging and still struggling actors mostly, who will tell you he is the greatest actor alive. If you have lunch with them in the Edison Hotel coffee shop just off Broadway, they will name a dozen productions with which even the most ardent theatergoers would be unfamiliar, productions that transpired over the years in cramped spaces on dark side streets, without pay or publicity, for runs of just one week or at most two. They will dive inward to salvage for you those long-sunken performances only to resurface a minute later, gasping for air, unable to bring it back with them and saddened by the irrecuperability of the theatrical event. If only he'd done movies, they will say, but knowing it wouldn't have been the same. On the stage he materialized with the lights and stood stiffly, tensely in place, precisely the kind of thing that isn't supposed to be done. The space charged and crackled around him, and he was no longer a man or even an actor but now a kind of fractured mirror, and what the audience members saw was themselves, in the midst of unfathomable searches, struggling against the overwhelming inadequacies of the daily roles into which each of them had been thrown. They clung to his performance;

their lives depended on it. He carried them into an essential place, to the very heart of a work of art, and there is no place where life lives as true.

In the Edison, they will say Mory is what you call an actor's actor; and they may leave it at that. Or, they may say if you ever meet him, ask him to tell the story of his first role. This is a story he has related to me on a number of occasions, and perhaps it does explain some things.

At the time, a child had not yet been conceived, but something else had been. In a girl named Rochelle he had planted the seed of a dream, for her to nurture. The dream was of itself, the dream, budding, blossoming and spreading like a benign fire to the far horizons, far enough to brighten all the dreaming lives of the world. And so they eloped and moved to New York City, where dreams have long been known to flourish.

They arrived at Port Authority with two suitcases and two years' savings; neither of them had ever seen anything as forbidding as this vast and squalid station; lost souls with hung faces and bags in hand trundled in the low corridors and slumped against the dingy tiles, as if they had given up hope of escaping the terminal and knew the brightest light they would see again was the sparkle of booze in tipped bottles.

The apartment he found was in the area of Manhattan known as Hell's Kitchen. He didn't tell her what the neighborhood was called, just that it was on the West Side, not far from the Hudson, and only a few blocks from the theaters of Broadway. When the cab stopped, Rochelle didn't want to get out. There were hard-eyed boys with greasy hair sitting on the stoops, old men in undershirts and women with cigarettes in their mouths leaning from the windows. The cab moved off, stranding them on the curb.

When she saw the apartment, Rochelle began to softly cry and Morpheus didn't know what to do. Somehow he hadn't noticed the mess before. The air was stale and the walls were smudged with the umber residue of years of smoke. Crushed cigar butts and desiccated insect carcasses littered the splintering wood floor and window sills. Live roaches scuttled around mouse droppings on the faded, torn linoleum of the kitchen. The bathroom was filmed with a grayish scum of soap, dust and hair. She didn't understand how he could have chosen this place. He was thinking about how to console her when from the apartment above them they heard a couple begin to shout at each other. They stood frozen in the front room for the duration of the fight. Rochelle fished a tissue from her handbag and blew her nose.

She was sick; she said it was an allergy, but whether it was to the remnants of a household pet, the dust, pollen in the air, she didn't know. Morpheus bought a day bed and put it next to the front window, and she lay in it for a week without leaving the apartment. Her allergy medicine made her drowsy; when she wasn't sleeping, she sat up and stared out the window, down through the bars of the fire escape at the senseless activity on the street below.

Morpheus plunged into the active city. He circulated headshots and vitae to agencies in bright, faceless buildings; he scanned the trade papers; he haunted the bulletin boards of the actors' guilds. He kept moving. He walked around Times Square, reading the marquees. He walked up and down the trails of Central Park, studying scripts for open-call auditions. He walked downtown, along the Bowery, through Little Italy and Chinatown and the Lower East Side. He walked and walked; each day he outwalked the boundaries of the day before. His feet walked and his identity flowed through the sluices of streets and souls. Lost in the crowds, he would become whatever character the next audition required him to be. If there were no auditions, he would follow people. He trailed a ragged old man with a wilted flower tucked behind his ear. He mimicked the old man's hesitant step, stooping posture, the squint of his eyes, the way his head swiveled to one side to spit. Morpheus limped and squinted and spat all the way down Second Avenue, and the patterns of the body led to patterns of the mind, until the infinite wall between them wavered and vanished and never was, and he felt he was the old man, every step pricked with a thousand reveries and regrets. He went back home elated, suffused with his powers. He jumped onto the bed where his wife lay drugged and half-dreaming. He pulled her up and pointed her toward the window.

"By the time I'm twenty-five," he said, "I'm going to own this city."

In his arms he felt her sigh.

"Well then you'll be the greatest slumlord alive," she said.

Her voice was a dreary wave. He shook it off, laughed softly. "There's more to it than West Forty Sixth Street, you know."

"I suppose I wouldn't."

"It's much more, Shel. It's everything. Our lives can mean something here."

"You mean we meant nothing before?"

"No. I just meant...we meant less. We mean more now."

He felt her relaxing into him. Her voice was still cheerless, but soft now too. "I'm glad to hear it," she said.

From the apartment upstairs the shouts came again. They could hear the voices clearly through the open window.

—*I'm washed up. You hear me? I'm washed up. You better just kill me and get it over with.*

—*That's right, Lou. That's right. I should just put you out of your misery, right?*

—*That's right.*

—*Well maybe I will. Maybe I'll put you out of my misery.*

—*Might as well.*

—*Well not today. Today you're outta luck.*

—*Outta luck. You said it.*

Morpheus and Rochelle looked up and followed the sound of boots trudging across the ceiling. A door opened and shut; the boots trudged down the steps past their landing; through the window, they watched the man trudge off down the street. The upstairs couple had become a source of amusement, speculation and slight contention. Morpheus judged them to be about fifteen years older, but Rochelle said it had to be more like twenty-five; she couldn't bear the thought of a mere fifteen years ravaging a couple so much. Lou was a wiry man, scrappier than Morpheus, with similar though more haunted features. His dark eyes were more recessed and closer set, his oily skin darker, creased and worn. Fiona, his wife, had curled, graying hair and a shocked look to her face. She wore shapeless housedresses that looked like she made them herself. Lou, they had learned, worked in the sewers. One time Fiona complained about the way he smelled when he came home from work and he growled back, *get with it honey, it's eau de toilette, and it's all the rage in France,* and Morpheus and Rochelle had to struggle not to laugh too loudly. They began to compare notes on the couple. Rochelle talked about having to listen to the soap operas

Fiona watched. Morpheus told her how he had tracked Lou through the streets. He imitated for her the man's swaggering walk, the way his arms billowed out in front of him as if his girth were twice what it was, the way his feet splayed, the way he rubbed his hands, gritted his crooked teeth and whistled through the gaps.

Morpheus brought home a used television, so Rochelle could see the soaps as well as hear them. At night they ate TV dinners and watched some of the prime-time shows, the ones shot in New York. And then she would sleep and he would sit out on the fire escape, smoking cigarette after cigarette and waiting for dawn to break grainily over the street below, at which point he could manage to drift off for a while. All the walking he did during the days didn't help; he couldn't get to sleep until morning. At first it didn't worry him. He was too excited for sleep; daydreams kept his mind racing all night. But as the weeks passed without work, excitement gave way to anxiety, and fantasies of success transformed into phantasms of failure, and still he couldn't sleep; until one night, looking down through the spectral grillwork of the fire escape, his frazzled mind peopled the empty street with shades; they rose up from the gutters, the souls of all the countless millions whose lives had passed through the City, to circulate anonymously as they had in life, leaving behind nothing but an unmeasurably slight erosion and residue, the thin silt of sidewalks and soles that blackened the gutters. That day he had spotted the man with the flower tucked in his ear, staggering down Canal Street, muttering to himself. Captivated, Morpheus trailed him once again. What could have made this man the wretch that he was, so destitute there were holes in his shoes, so alone there was no one to talk to but himself? Morpheus allowed the transformation to begin. He felt his vision cloud, bile in the back of his throat, calluses on his feet, a submerged terror and the need to hear his own voice, his last possession. Morpheus got closer to hear the words, and saw the old man wasn't as old as he'd thought. "Ay!" he was saying, with a wild fling of his arm. "Every inch a king! When I do stare, see how the subject quakes." With a numb terror, Morpheus recognized the words as King Lear's. He stopped, and as the man disappeared and the crowd shifted and reeled around him, Morpheus suddenly perceived the whole city to be filled with actors, trailing one another endlessly, each one imagining himself the sole heir to a dream impressed upon them all by some inhuman force. He looked up at the jumble of walls and windows and saw the city as a monstrous trap, to which they were all irresistibly drawn, coming by the thousands to pile their aspirations one atop the other, resulting in something unprecedentedly grotesque. The city, he saw, was a massive by-product of untold thousands of impossible dreams.

Morpheus tried drinking, at night, to help his mind rest. But it worked only for a few days, after which he was left half-awake and half-drowned by the dark spirits flowing through him, and the dawn found him washed up on his barren perch. What amount of talent, what amount of time, what amount of sacrifice did it take to make something great of a life? These were the questions, on such nights, that passed through his mind.

One day another actor in the Edison gave him some pills, and that was how his barbiturate addiction began. He took two pills every night to help him sleep. He took half a pill before auditions to soothe his growing fear of failure. And one pill during the afternoon when the crowds began to get to him.

Morpheus stopped going out every day. He stayed home with Rochelle and the two of them slept into the afternoon, she with her allergy pills, he with his Quaaludes. The ensuing weeks passed silently, cloudily, like a long, overcast afternoon in which nothing could hope to happen. It seemed things would go on this way indefinitely, and it wouldn't have surprised either of them to wake up on some gray afternoon decades later, to part the gauze of sheets and listless dreams and discover that they had slept their lives away. One day while they slept, someone came in off the fire escape through the open window, picked up the television, and walked back out. Morpheus woke up and saw the vacant shelf. He looked at his sleeping wife, trying to decide whether or not to wake her. Hovering over her repose he saw how young she was and how beautiful she was, and was overcome with the feeling that it was he himself who was the thief; he had crept into her childhood and lulled her with his dreams of New York, and while she dreamed he had made off with her life. And now with a sense of helpless inevitability he woke her and told her of the theft, and she sat up and the mist of her dream cleared, and they fought, and she told him he was a liar, a liar, not an actor, just a liar, or what's the difference anyway, and he put on his clothes, about to storm out of the apartment when from upstairs the couple started shouting again.

—*You can't go, Lou. I can't stand it!*

—*I gotta go! You know I gotta go. It's time and a half for chrissakes! And besides. They need me. It's my duty.*

—*It aint your duty. You don't owe nobody.*

—*I owe lots.*

They listened to him trudge down the stairs. They watched him trudge down the street.

It was the last argument Lou and Fiona ever had. He didn't come home from work that day, or any other. At night they could hear Fiona crying by the window. Eventually her cries found words. *Lou,* she would say. *Come back. Please come back. Oh God. Let him come back.* The prayer was repeated every night. They learned from another neighbor that Lou had died in a sewer accident. He was repairing a section of wall that collapsed and swept him out into the Hudson along with several tons of untreated sewage. His body had not been recovered. Fiona refused to make arrangements for a service. She refused to believe he was dead.

One night, kept from sleep by the woman's hopeless wailing, Rochelle propped herself up in bed.

"I should go up there," she said.

Morpheus rolled onto his back. "Why?"

"We're neighbors."

"This is New York. We've got ten million neighbors." Morpheus reached for her but she was already out of the bed.

Morpheus sat by the window feeling uneasy. He heard their voices without being able to make out the words. There were long silences. He began to think about the dead man. He felt guilty for the times he'd aped Lou's movements for Rochelle, to amuse her, to show off. Turning it over though, he realized that Lou might be preserved, in this small way at least, in his own body's memory. He jumped up and did Lou's walk around the dark apartment, legs slightly bowed, short steps slapping on the floor as if unaccustomed to walking. He plodded in circles, in spirals, he spun, arms held out in front as though counterbalancing a pregnancy. But for all the mannerisms the man was not invoked. There was too much missing. Morpheus had been able to fool himself into thinking he knew strangers on the street, but Lou was slightly more than a stranger. The failure shouldn't have been surprising, but it overwhelmed him all the same. Rochelle came back down to find him standing in the middle of the floor, staring at his feet.

"It's so sad," said Rochelle. Morpheus pointed to the open window and motioned for her to whisper.

"What happened?" he said.

"Nothing. We drank tea," she said, and sat down on the bed. "The apartment was filled with those things — I don't know what they're called — the little glass balls with water in them and a monument, and when you turn it over it snows. There were hundreds of them."

"Hundreds?"

She nodded. "It's what Lou used to do. He started a company. They were all of New York. The Statue of Liberty. The Brooklyn Bridge. The Empire State Building. Radio City. The best were the ones with the whole skyline. They were so intricate."

"What happened to the company?"

"Oh. She told me. I can't remember."

"Come on. Think. What happened?"

The urgency in his voice elicited from her a strange look. "It was something legal," she said. "He didn't have the rights to the monuments. Something like that. He had to stop making them and he lost all his money."

"That's rotten," he muttered.

"We walked around turning them over.... It's the way she prays."

What happened over the next few weeks is more difficult to piece together. Morpheus always skips over this part entirely, so here I rely on Rochelle's recollections. The visit with Fiona had shaken her. Sitting with the worn-down, grieving woman in that apartment shaped exactly like her own, Rochelle had the chilling sensation of peering into a crystal ball and seeing her own future. When she went to bed she even dreamed of that future, dreamed of waking up as if from a twenty-year coma in an apartment filled with glass balls, next to an empty space in the bed, and looking into the mirror and seeing a face that was only a shadow of her own, with hair that was curled and gray.

She woke early, Morpheus asleep beside her. She got up and stared at the tangle of white sheets that threatened to drain her life away. She decided to go for a walk.

She began to go out every day and quickly lost her fear of the city. She bought things for the apartment, no longer worrying about their dwindling savings. She bought decorations, plants of all kinds, a window box with flowers. She went out to buy fabric, but thought of Fiona's frumpy homemade dresses, and instead bought herself a designer pantsuit. Morpheus didn't complain; he barely even noticed. Telling herself it was to test him, she brought home stranger and more expensive things, a tapestry with unicorns, a brocade bedspread, a bronze candelabra. But he made no comments. He just nodded and slipped back into reading, pacing, or just a brooding trance. She told herself that she would get a job soon, but not yet. She needed to be outside in the sunlight, to feel like things were possible once again.

Morpheus didn't make it easy. He had lost all concern for his appearance; he stopped shaving and his clothes seemed to get filthier by the day, mottled with dark stains. He began to talk about sports, something he'd never shown the slightest interest in; he looked through the paper and cursed certain teams and rattled off statistics. And then there were the tics, which he seemed to accumulate daily. He ran a worried hand over the top of his head, wrinkled his brow, drummed fingers on the tabletop. For the first time it struck her that prior to this Morpheus had had no tics at all. He had never tapped his foot when music was in the air. He had never sighed in the midst of a long silence, chewed on the end of a pen, played with his food or idly folded his napkin at a meal. And now he was doing all these things and more, and his face, normally calm and dark, had become a chaotic palette of expressions, daubed with anguish, rage, or senseless mirth.

Rochelle could not confront him. She was struggling for her life while he was sinking without protest, and she wasn't strong enough to pull him out of the sloth as well. She had to save herself. She didn't ask him about auditions. They rarely talked at all, except for after her nightly tea with Fiona, when he tended to rouse himself, asking all sorts of questions, satisfied only when he thought he'd milked out every drop of information. The endless stories about Lou were as enthralling to him as they were hateful to her. Rochelle had kept going up there because the sound of Fiona's crying was so pitiful, and also because she hoped the constant sight of Fiona would strengthen her resolve to avoid the future this woman represented. But it was taxing. She felt like Fiona and Morpheus were in league to suffocate her, pressing themselves like great pillows from either side.

One night she watched him pace around the room, feet bumping absently into furniture. She was shocked by how old he looked, and fought the impulse to run to the mirror to see if she too had aged.

"It's time for your visit," he said. He scratched his ribcage through his undershirt.

"I'm not going tonight," she said.

"But honey! You gotta go. She's expecting you, aint she?"

"Mory," she said, the realization coming as she spoke. "Why are you acting like the dead man?"

Morpheus did not answer. Even if he had revealed to her his plan, he knew it wouldn't have answered the question. What was it about Lou that compelled him? He was never able to explain this, to Rochelle, or to me. I believe he saw himself in that man. Lou also had come to the city with a dream, and had sized things up and astutely surmised that the city was awash with dreams, and most would come to nothing; but dreams themselves were a commodity that would always be in demand. He designed a product that would cater to those city dreams, and thereby make his own come true. But the brutal lesson he learned was that the dreamer is not the owner of his dream; those rights are an exclusive property — of the city itself.

"Morpheus," she said, an undercurrent of fear swelling in her voice. "Where do you go during the day?"

He looked at her as if she were a bright object removed an unbridgeable distance, and responded in a deadened voice: "The sewers."

The next night he was ready to enact his plan. Rochelle could barely believe the transformation. Waking from a long after-dinner nap, she discovered him in the bathroom with his makeup kit, sitting on the toilet and looking into a round mirror propped on the sink. There was hair all over the tile floor, and the top of his head was nearly bare, with long strands plastered over one side. The skin of his face and arms was a bluish white and his eyes were ringed by deep gray caverns. He had changed the thickness of his nose and penciled his teeth with angular shadows. He stood up and hitched a leather workbelt around his waist.

"You'll find some powder in a Baggie on the counter," he said. It's a couple of pills I've crushed up. When you make the tea, slip this into hers. It will help the effect."

After the wave of horror, to her surprise what Rochelle felt most was relief; the tension that had been building inexorably over the last few weeks suddenly broke; it was madness, that was clear, but there was method in it. She approached him, taking in the details — the low balance of his stance, the crook of his arms, the peculiar rictus of his mouth. She was awed by how convincing he was.

"Do you really think you can do it?"

"If I can," he said, "I'm the greatest actor this town will ever see."

She kissed his blue lips, and went upstairs.

A half hour later, she returned. He stood up slowly, lifted the toilet seat, and scooped fouled water into a mop bucket. He stepped into the bathtub, raised the bucket over his head and poured the liquid onto himself, reaching down to recover some feces from the tub to smear on his arms and pantlegs. Stiff as a sleepwalker, he moved across the apartment to the window. He looked back at his wife in the doorway, and clambered out onto the fire escape.

Silently, he ascended. The block was asleep. A few empty windows were still lit, rectangles of uneven light in the airy dark. He stepped onto Fiona's landing. As he knew it would be, the window was open. She would see his legs first, and then look up and see the rest of him obscured through the doubled windows between the parting of the curtains. She was slumped on the sofa, watching the TV with half-closed eyes. He had never seen her this close before, and yet she was the most familiar sight in his life. He wanted to step in and smooth the lines of worry from her face, for at once he saw her old and young, a widow and a brand new bride, and his heart was stabbed with a pang of tenderness and triumph. Through the tears forming in his eyes, he took in the room around her, full of their miniature visions of New York, submerged in water, sealed in glass. They lay on top of the TV, on the mantle, the dining room table, and along every shelf of a glass-doored cabinet, glittering in the low flickering light of the television.

Her eyes rolled toward him, widened. She gasped with difficulty and her hand rose to her mouth. Her feet shuffled on the floor, trying to stand. He held up his hand to stop her movements.

"I've come," he said in a hoarse husk of a voice, "so you can see the truth."

She was unable to speak, but he saw her lips take the form of a kiss, forming his name. "Lou," she mouthed.

"I died, Fiona, like I lived. Fighting a river of shit." He allowed his face a skeletal smile.

"...no," the woman said, "...I'm dreaming..."

"Sure, baby, sure. Who aint dreaming?" He winked.

"Lou..." Her lips puckered into his name, and then fluttered, as down her face tears rolled, small rolling worlds of bluish light.

This is the story of my father's first role, the story of how he became an artist, constructing a truth from the material of a fabulous lie. He told it many times as I grew up. The tellings themselves have undergone a transformation over the years; with every relation, something new was revealed. Time was required for both of us to grow into certain aspects of the story. Only recently have I been old enough to hear and has he been ready to relate the role that barbiturates played, in that performance, and subsequently in his life. Somewhere in the course of my childhood, that particular drug gave way to others — marijuana, heroin, and then lithium, Desipramine, Prozac, and most recently, Zoloft. He says the latter has given him a new outlook on life, a calmness, an ability to face the disappointments and frustrations of his career with a kind of equanimity. He calls it wisdom; but looking into his eyes as he tells me this I see a gauze of clouds, and listening to the intonation of his voice I hear a hollow stirring wind, and I am skeptical.

And as he shuts his eyes and drifts off in his chair, I stand over him and think about where he is drifting. I see him seeing himself once again preparing for the role, descending from the hopeful sunlight to wade through the murky current of the sewers, among the shades of city dwellers past, picturing himself everywhere among them. His artistry had led him beyond life and into another realm, a journey from which he could not fully return. He was never quite the same again, as my mother will tell you if you ask. His dreams did not set fire to the world, but took root in a secret hothouse, a patch of bright poppies to aid his dim repose. I am twenty-three years old, the age of my father when all this began. As I grow older, time may add to or it may erase the things I know. Perhaps when I am forty-eight, as my father is now, much of what he told me will be irrelevant, buried or forgotten altogether, and most of the intricacies of the various tellings will have merged into a single shadowy form, a mere ghost of a meaning. But the very first telling, I am certain, will remain just where it has stood since my seventh birthday, a stark monument at the center of my consciousness. I see him now as he told it then, leaning over my bed, hands smelling of smoke resting on either side of my pillowed head, and from the storm in his eyes and the howling wind in his voice I now see he was heavily drugged that night.

"And what happened then?" Morpheus was asked by his seven year-old son.

"And then," said Morpheus, "Fiona saw Lou in her dreams. And the next morning, when she woke up, she knew that he was dead. Her crying woke me up. Rain was drumming on the fire escape and on the sill, and above, her feet thudded across the ceiling as she ran around her room, and I heard those glass balls shatter as she hurled them against the walls. Then the door slammed and she raced down the stairs. I jumped into some clothes and followed her out onto the street. She was running in the downpour. At the corner she knelt where the gutter stream cleaned the dirt and butts and garbage down through the bars of a sewer grate. She was peering in, and then she spotted something and screamed. A change came over her. Her head disappeared through the open slot above the grate, and her body scrabbled down after, frantically. The soaked hem of her housedress was the last thing to go, slipping down with a crisp flicker. I was close enough to hear the splash, and by the time I reached the grate, the change was complete; she was an alligator; the deep, undulating ridges of her back shone like jewels as she swam sleekly to the far shore of the dark underground river, where the corpse of her husband had washed up on the bank. She crawled up beside the drowned man and tried to warm his face with her lipless kisses. The edge of the river's current began to nuzzle his head toward hers, and his blue lips, green now, began to smile, and his crooked teeth multiplied as the smile spread all the way across his face until it was the biggest, widest, shit-eating grin this city has ever seen, and he too was now an alligator, and the two of them swam off down the rich, cascading river. And to this day, the alligators live in the sewers, happy and fulfilled; they are famed and feared, and every day the black waters provide them with a feast, of sewer workers, straying children, unwanted dogs and cats and babies, rats and pigeons, bums and suicides. They gorge themselves on the ruin and refuse of all the hopeless dreamers above, and they never lack food."

He never ended the story this way again. But that night, his voice, callous, embittered, seeped into my brand new mind and burned channels down which his age old doubts would begin to flow. I fight these doubts every day of my life. My father doesn't approve of my being a musician. He says he is afraid I will turn out like him, worn out by a chimerical life and a yawning death. Half joking, I told him by the time I'm twenty-five, the whole city would be singing my songs, and from his inward distance he looked at me, sad and tender and guilt-ridden and proud, as if I too were one of his fabulous constructions. But I have powers of my own, and whatever comes of my music, I'll know that I tried, and that I tried despite every indication of the futility of the attempt, and that I'm not giving in, not to life, not to death, and I'm never calling it all a mistake, and I'm never sleeping it all away, and I'm never looking back.

A CHANGE OF
HEART

Carl Cadwallater, millionaire, walked into the the Babybar and looked around. Dated plastic toys filled the shelves along the walls. In place of booths, a row of cribs jutted from the far wall, occupied mostly by dazed young men with sparse goatees who sucked apathetically on baby bottles and watched cartoons on the mounted televisions. The volume was muted, but in its place Chipmunk music grated the air like an iron comb. The bartender was bald, fat and shirtless. His pudgy, stubbled face, at first simply shocking, upon continued viewing became shockingly absurd. Carl couldn't help smiling, at which point the face soured and puckered and was even more amusing. Carl approached and the bartender backed off automatically. Resting his elbows on the bar and leaning forward, he discovered the bartender to be wearing nothing but an enormous disposable diaper. Carl laughed out loud. He discovered he enjoyed laughing, and kept it up until he was dizzy, while the bartender rested crossed arms on his paunch and scowled.

Carl let out a satisfied sigh. "This your place?" he asked.

"That's right," the bartender said, pressing two fingers down hard against a nicotine patch affixed to a shaved area of skin just over his heart.

"What's your name?"

"Barry."

"Barry," Carl repeated. "Barry the Baby." He laughed until his stomach ached. Barry bit his lip, tapped his bare toes on the rubber floor mat. "Sorry," Carl said. "Sorry, Barry. My name's Carl." He offered his hand, and finding Barry's hand limp, gripped it like a vise. "So, Barry, this is quite a little operation you've got going here. You make any dough from it?"

"A little."

"A labor of love, huh?"

"That's right."

"A little Gerber money, eh? Extra helping of strained peas now and then, huh? That must be nice." He hadn't planned to brag, but he couldn't help himself. "Barry," he said, leaning further over the bar. "Do you know how much money I made today?"

Barry looked around for other customers, gnawing and sucking on a thumbnail.

"You give up? I made a million dollars today. Sold short. Company went belly-up. Rolled over and died. I'm a rich man, Barry. I waited and I waited and I saw my chance and I pounced. A million dollars. You know how much that is?"

Barry said nothing.

"No, I guess not," Carl went on. "Math comes a couple years after potty training. Well, trust me Barry. It's a damn lot."

"No cussing," Barry said. "I don't allow any cussing in my place, all right?"

"Oh. Yeah, sure. Listen. I want a drink. Got any champagne? Or..." he said, pointing to Barry's sagging chest and struggling to contain his amusement, "...maybe you just breast-feed your customers?"

Barry's whole head turned pink like a half-sucked fireball and his clenched fists whitened. "Just leave it to me," he muttered. "I'll fix you up something real special." He pirouetted like a sumo ballerina and waddled away, his hairy flanks drooping over the huge swath of white plastic.

A woman walked in and took a seat down the bar. She had green-tinted hair, matted and on the way to dredlocked, a green motorcycle jacket covered with silver chains that wrapped around one shoulder, and something shining on her full, lower lip, which in the dim light Carl at first took for a bead of spittle but soon discerned as jewelry, a thin, silver ring. She chatted with the bartender while he agitated a drink shaker shaped like a baby's rattle. Carl couldn't make out the words, but Barry was clearly in fawning mode, with a shapeless yet definitely obsequious smile; and she seemed to be encouraging him, laughing and tossing her tangle of hair so it struck her back like a frayed leather whip. As the bartender poured out two drinks into baby bottles, she took off her jacket, revealing a red halter-top which she filled nicely. Then she turned toward Carl and gave him a long, playful look while, to Carl's continued amusement, the giant baby fumed, jealousy written all over his beetling brow and bulging underlip. He took the drinks under the bar, and...from where Carl sat, it looked like he might be pissing in them, but his diaper didn't seem constructed for such an operation.

Carl peered into the recess of his wallet as the bartender approached with a sound of plastic and chafing skin.

"Barry," he said. "You're gonna love this. I'm ah... a little light tonight. But hey, you know I'm good for it, right?"

"Sure, Carly," Barry said, his mush of a smile presiding over a squat temple of fingers. "This one's on me."

Carl sucked his bottle and watched the woman suck hers, her lips teasing the rubber nipple and leaving behind a bright red smudge. A greenish tattoo, the design of which he couldn't make out, spanned her shoulderblades. There was a flash of smooth skin between her yellow skirt and over-the-knee stockings as she shifted on her perch, re-crossing her legs. She might even be a beautiful woman, he decided, if her hair were combed out, re-dyed, and deloused maybe, and the lip ring and the dozen earrings and studs were done away with. He felt sorry for her. She was probably one of those nice girls from a small town who move to the city, seduced by glamour magazines, only to be transformed, step by step, into urban savages, modern primitives, whatever they called it. This city devoured people by the millions, enslaved them in its stinking bowels. He thought of his former self, straphanger, rent-payer, Whopper-eater, holder of phone between shoulder and neck, dictionary definition of *schmuck*. Today, his years of waiting and plotting had paid off. Tomorrow he would get on a plane and fly away, to a place without pavement or car horns or skyscrapers. The image coalesced in his mind. It was a beast, this city, a freak monster with concrete scales, bristling spines and piercing horns, and he had mastered it, taken its treasure. A million in the bank. He would live on a mountaintop, call his brokerage now and then and watch as the city put its giant green back to work for him.

He was still staring at the girl; he felt he understood her. She was one of those who had not escaped, who probably never would. Underneath all the metal rings and dirty hair, there was a troubled girl with touchingly simple needs: a little respect, a sense of order, and a way out of this hell.

For a moment he was surprised by the breadth of his thoughts, which struck him as not a little profound. But it felt so natural, here in the bar tonight, a million dollars richer. His senses, he perceived, were growing more acute with each passing minute. He could sympathize with this girl living in her stylized slum. His hands, he noticed, were caressing the wood of the bar, and even through the glaze of countless wipings and polishings he could feel the intricate texture of the grain. That was what it was like, his new feeling, penetrating the glaze, a new laser-sharp focus on life. He felt like a god. He stared at the girl. She was beautiful, he knew it now, and it was something that not even she knew, he could see that too, the way her suddenly hollow eyes fled from his, the way she was now hunching down into the shadows, digging ragged nails into her arms, and he would wade into the quagmire that her life had become, pull her out, clean her up, and redeem her, and she would thank him with her heart.

Barry the bartender cast surreptitious glances to either side as he leaned over the sink, reaching into the shelf under the bar to stopper up his two tiny vials, one green and the other red. Barry always took great pains to give his customers what they needed. The Xtacy was taking its toll on Mr. Suit-and-tie, and the little teaser was clawing herself apart; the LSD was making her withdrawn and paranoid. Barry was aware that some people considered him to be a bit obsessive about his work. He preferred to think of himself as a perfectionist. It was, after all, a labor of love. He smiled at Carl and Carl grinned back dreamily. He smiled at the girl and her eyes snapped down to the bar.

Laura Lambert had come out to unwind after spending the day with her father, an old wizard who lived in a high-rise tower in the Bronx. She had grown up in that apartment, which seemed smaller every time she returned. They were sitting in their habitual chairs by the window when he finally dropped the questions all at once, leaning forward to set his coffee down with a clatter on the table. Why had she gone to college if all she was going to do was wait tables? When was she going to give him a son-in-law, a grandchild? When would she settle on one path and stick to it? What did she want to do? What did she want from life?

She had gazed out the window down at the twin rivers side by side, one, the Harlem River, of metallic water, and the other, the Deegan Expressway, of flowing metal. She told him she wanted to be immersed in life, and at the same time safe from it, high and dry. She told him that she wanted to live and she wanted not to live. She shifted in her chair that now felt uncomfortable because her feet could touch the floor. She told him that she couldn't settle into anything, because what she wanted was change, to change and keep changing forever.

The answer troubled him, she could tell, but there was indulgence in his aqueous gaze. She knew that he would do anything for her, anything she asked. When she was young she'd believed he could do anything at all. He was an amateur magician, and throughout her childhood had produced gifts from handkerchiefs waved in the air: candy, costume jewelry, a rabbit, a canary. As a child, she had witnessed her mother's life being taken by a speeding cab, along with what would have been her younger sister or brother yet to be born. Her father had been a cab driver himself, but around the time of her mother's death he became a dispatcher, the position he still held. He had spoiled her as best he could, because something had to make up for the lack of a mother, and because in any event it would have been against his nature to do otherwise.

Laura was now treating herself to a night of bar and club hopping. It was the only activity that felt right to her.

On nights like this the city sidled up to her like an intimate friend and guided her on paths of warm and gemmy light. The Babybar was a natural choice to start the evening. It fit in with the theme of the day; whenever she saw her father she came away with that childlike feeling of being small, almost insignificant in the scheme of things, but at the same time precious, protected, full of the knowledge that what she said and what she did and every change of heart would be heeded as solemnly as a law.

This bar was the most unthreatening place in the city. But somehow everything in it was looking more and more sinister. On the television, a cartoon dog smoked a stick of dynamite he'd taken for a cigar and was transmuted into a big black ash with eyes. On a shelf, two decrepit rag dolls joined by long hugging arms now seemed to be tearing the stuffing out of each other. She glanced over at the man with the briefcase she had smiled at before, and he was fixing her with a crazed grin like he was about to eat her alive. She looked away and saw the bald bartender, leering as he hitched his diapers below his jostling paunch. She thought about her father wanting grandchildren and envisioned her belly swollen with this two-hundred-fifty-pound, fur-backed baby. The bottles loomed on the shelf before her, dozens of cold, craven phalluses. She clutched her flat stomach to reassure herself.

"Hi."

She flinched, almost tipping her barstool. The man with the briefcase was standing next to her. She felt vulnerable on the stool, a pedestal raised for all to see. She crossed her arms by reflex, but the feel of her own flesh made her flinch again.

"My name's Carl. I made a million dollars today." It was, he figured, potentially his one and only chance to use this line. As she sat hunched over herself, he studied the tattoo on her back, a single sinuous wing stretching from shoulder to shoulder, over which her head was turned, staring at him with wide, green eyes, which then narrowed.

"You spent the whole day doing that?"

For a moment Carl was reduced to silence. "Yes...I guess I did." He thought about the years he'd spent networking, kissing ass, gathering information, all the false starts and sleepless nights and nervewracking risks and trials of patience, waiting for this day. And now, facing the most beautiful woman he'd ever seen, he felt like it had all been a waste of time. It had come between them, made him give her that awful line. He astonished himself by thinking that at this moment he would give up as much as a quarter, no, as much as *half* the money, just for the chance to press his ear to her chest, listen to the warm rhythm of her heart, assure himself that she was in fact a living creature. He noticed the outline of a nipple ring on her left breast.

"Can I ask you a personal question?" he said.

"God, no." His face was too vivid and complicated to look at. She stared at his red tie, a slick, hanging tongue. She looked away.

"I was just wondering how you kiss. I mean with that ring in your lip."

"Some things you were never meant to know."

"Not all fabulously rich men are jerks, you know."

"Just my luck I'd find one who is." He wanted something from her, and his stare threatened to take it at any moment; and all she had to stand in his way were these words, forged in the furnace of her mouth, around the silver stud in her tongue; one by one they came out perfect, each one a hard sparkling diamond for her to spit.

With words Carl rarely felt in his element. Everything he said made him sound like an asshole, which he knew judging from what was said back to him. But he was in an incredible mood, and he saw beneath her words like he saw beneath her urban armor of leather and rings. He saw through all the way to her fragile soul. He would get past the words; it had to be this way, the strength of this newfound love would prevail. He felt the waves of it, a suffusing physical pleasure, rising up from his heart, emanating from him. It would penetrate the armor. She would feel it too. He moved closer to her and the scent of her perfume almost made him faint.

"Do you mind?" she said.

"How could I?" he said.

"Excuse me but I've got to be somewhere you're not and I'm running late." Laura jumped off the stool, struggled into her jacket and walked quickly out the door. The ceaseless street activity, usually so reassuring, now stabbed icicles of dread from every direction. At the corner, she stopped and watched the furious river of yellow taxis coursing by. She couldn't cross. It was terrifying and impersonal, a flood of sperm rampaging through a pliable womb. She looked away from the traffic and was gradually soothed by the city light: warm light from windows, far-off winking lights of aircraft, streetlights sprinkling pixie-dust that floated down to eddy on the sidewalks around the shuffle of shoes and random currents of air. The city was a place of wise magic, and the night was an open invitation. Her hand was on her chest, she noticed, and her heartbeat had calmed. She closed her eyes and breathed the night air.

There was a hand on her shoulder. She spun around. It was *him,* his head jutting forward with a lopsided smile. She'd forgotten to get away, she'd been just standing like a statue at the corner.

"I was afraid I'd lost you. But you waited for me." Carl watched her face; in the initial shock, her hand had shot up to cover her open mouth, fingers ringed by big, imitation stones—ruby, topaz, emerald; and her eyebrows had forged an adorable little crease on her brow, a miracle he was intensely grateful to have lived to see.

"Waiting for you to drop dead," Laura replied. The man's face was a frightening machine of expression. He didn't seem to be aware of his own existence. His eyes floated in a dreamy vacuum. "I want to be alone," she said with a touch of desperation. Her legs started working again, propelling her away.

"Can I walk with you a while?"

The city seeped in around Carl as she walked off, her yellow skirt a swaying buoy in a shipwrecking sea, round, bright and welcoming, high and dry atop the determined gait of her long glimmering legs, each step celebrated by a bootsplash on the puddled sidewalk. Had she been truly walking on water he couldn't have been more enthralled, and there was nothing to do but follow in her wake. He caught up, trotting and capering at her side. For something to say, he said, "This neighborhood is terrible, you know. If something happened to you it would be my fault. I couldn't stand it."

"The neighborhood is fine."

She seemed offended, and Carl started to backpedal. "Yeah, sure, it's probably no worse than any other in this city."

"What's wrong with this city?"

Now he could no longer contain himself. "What isn't wrong with it? Everybody's unhappy and alone. Nobody trusts anyone. This city...it does things to people. Haven't you noticed? It changes people. It changed me. I never thought about money before I came here. And look what it's done to you."

"What do you mean?"

He couldn't tell her what he meant. "One day it'll swallow you up. That would be a tragedy."

"It would be beautiful."

"You're beautiful."

"Where's a cab when you need it?" Laura said. But she didn't mean it. Tonight the cabs were scaring her even more than this man.

"You've got me all wrong," Carl said. "I'm not some crazed stalker. I'm not a rapist or a thug or a psycho. You're running away because this city is so full of creeps you've probably never met a normal guy like me." They came to a group of people crowding around a doorway. He felt the grvity of the bass and drums cause a lapping tide in his bone marrow. "I used to be normal, anyway. Before today. Now I'm even better than normal, because I'm rich." She slipped through the crowd and left him at the edge. "And I'm in love!" Heads turned to study him. Laura whispered something to the pock-faced, bearded bouncer, who nodded, looking at Carl. She disappeared into the club. He began to push through the crowd, but the bouncer crossed his huge arms and glared at him. It was hopeless. He turned back. He crossed the street, barely hearing the screaming horn of a taxi veering around him. He sat down on the opposite curb between two parked cars and watched the door.

In the club, Laura stood still in the middle of the dancing mob. A sweaty man knocked her down. She wiped her hands on her skirt, trying to get rid of the feeling of flesh but only intensifying the sensation. She was enmeshed in a web of eyes bobbing in the beams of light, sticking to every part of her body. She had to move. She found her way to the bathroom and stared at her reflection in the mirror. Could this be her? It couldn't. It wasn't her that the man in the suit was chasing. It was this thing in the mirror that was the cause of all her problems. She wasn't just a body. She didn't want or even need a body. She sensed this now, and it was like a revelation. She locked herself in a stall and stared at the shiny red toilet while around it the red tiles of the walls and floor did a crazed jig. She sat down on the fixture and grabbed a green beer bottle lying on the tiles. She struck it against the porcelain gullet between her legs. It made a shallow sound and didn't break. The second time it shattered, and in her fist was the jagged, translucent neck. She pulled down the low-cut front of her halter-top and etched with the sharpest edge of the glass a line on the inner side of her left breast where she imagined her heart would be. *More than a body,* she mouthed as she etched the line, at first white, and then red as she repeated the stroke with increasing force, *more than a body,* and then beads of red emerged, and with another stroke the blood began to trickle. She felt a grim triumph, but then she was feeling the pain and trying to stanch the cut, first with her hand, and then with a wad of toilet paper.

Carl sat on the curb, watching a rivulet of trash-filled water flow in the gutter under the creased bridges of his pantlegs; match books, bottlecaps, butts and bits of cellophane and paper careening by, a lilliputian parody of the traffic of the street. He looked up and the goon was still at the door, in the same position, legs spread, arms folded. Little by little, he let the crowd trickle in. The club was open to everyone but him. Carl realized that if he were someone else, anyone else, he would have a chance at the happiness now denied him.

Two kids in ripped tanktops and backwards hats were skateboarding on the wide sidewalk behind him.

"Listen," Carl said to the smarter-looking one. "How'd you like to make twenty bucks?"

The kid waited.

"Watch that door. If a woman comes out, a beautiful woman, with a face pale and radiant like a passing cloud, with a forest of green hair, and the look of a doe stunned by headlights in her big green eyes, watch which way she goes, and don't let her out of your sight. Okay?"

The kid seemed impressed. "Okay, sir," he said.

Carl ran around the corner and up two blocks to a bank machine. A one-armed man wearing a dirty red wool hat opened the door for him. Carl withdrew the maximum. He turned and stopped in the doorway.

"How much for the hat?" he said.

The old man stared at him; his mouth began to operate but no words came out.

Carl opened his wallet. "Here." He put two twenties in the man's callused palm and snatched the hat from his head, fitting it on his own as he ran back down the street.

Carl paid some suburban punk girls with sparkling makeup and multicolor hairdoes for a quick makeover. In a vestibule littered with crack vials, he traded his Italian suit for a three-card monte dealer's baggy green jeans. At a makeshift sidewalk bazaar of clothing, porno magazines and eight-track tapes, he bartered his briefcase, cell phone and portable fax for a yellow leather jacket with indecently large lapels.

The skatepunk didn't recognize Carl until he thrust a twenty into his hand.

"The woman. She leave?"

The kid shook his head. "No way. No one like that."

Carl smiled, gave the kid another twenty. "Spend it on a girl. Okay?"

"Okay, dude."

Carl sauntered across the street. The clothes seemed to dictate a new way of walking. He found a slow, easy bounce to his steps, stopping every now and then and salaaming to let a cab whiz by. He walked through the crowd and stared brazenly at the door thug, who looked back at him without recognition or interest.

"Can't let you in right now," the man grunted. "Too crowded."

"Oh," Carl said, nonchalant. He began to turn away and then spun back around. "Hey, I think I met you before." He held out his hand with a folded twenty stuck between two fingers. The man shook his hand.

"Yeah, that's right. Always good to see an old friend."

Carl paid the cashier and waded into the waves of motion and sound. This was the city within the city. Everything that was outside was here as well, and even more intensely. He had never understood these places before. Why would people want to come in from all the crowds and noise to a place of even more crowds and noise? Invariably, he had felt out of place. But now, adrift in the throbbing mass, he saw that everyone was out of place, like passengers jostling in a subway, each staring at some carefully selected neutral point and doing his best not to acknowledge the existence of any of the others. This comforted him. They all had something in common.

Strobelight flashed in the chamber, and the dancers winked in and out, in frozen, crook-limbed poses. And then he saw her, dancing not too far from where he stood, turning off and on with a kind of ease, as if this frantic indecisive light were her natural habitat; in one fragment of a second she was there, eyes wide and starkly questioning, and in the next she was out of the world. Carl watched with trepidation and awe, sensing that she could be lost any time and that each reappearance was an incredible piece of luck. He feared for her in this troubled plane where things teetered so precariously on the edge of oblivion; she belonged in a place of permanence, emblazoned by stars in changeless constellations, out beyond the arrogant babel of urban light. He moved through the dancers and stood opposite her; he bounced on his heels to the beat. Her eyes lit on him for a second and then fluttered onward; through his camouflage of rags and face paint he watched her with impunity, preserving the transitory flashes of her being. Her lips pursed. Hair mid-whirl. Ringed hands pressed in prayer. Full breasts frozen heaving. Rounded hip outswung. Hands on luminescent thighs. He took off his yellow leather jacket and dropped it on top of her biker jacket and grinned at the sight of their two jackets sprawled together on the floor between them, as though it were some voodoo rite that could not fail to bring about the mingling of their fates. Carl was dancing, for the first time in years. He was dancing with the woman he loved.

The strobe stopped and colored spots swung and flashed again, and in the relative constancy of the light, white fog from smoke machines rolled across the floor. Laura was exhilarated. In the strobelight, she had forgotten her body, forgotten herself, and had felt the secret order to the chaos. All the dancers were dancing as a single organism, giving themselves up to the rhythm of the light. And now, in the soft, post-coital color and fog, the world was shimmering and misted, a soul with wings. This was what the city could be like, she felt it now again and more than ever. She looked around to see if others were sharing the joy of the moment. She found herself sneaking glances at a guy in baggy jeans, dancing with crazed, flailing gestures of his arms and legs to a beat of his own imagining. Her eyes were drawn to his face, smeared with green sparkling mascara and blood red lipstick, like a clown from a circus in hell, his psychedelic raccoon eyes imploring her in a way that made her shudder and look away. She looked again. He smiled, a lopsided section of teeth. It couldn't be, but it was.

"Like the new threads?" he yelled into her ear. "My darling, you groove divinely. How 'bout me?"

She stood paralyzed, her fists locked in front of her as though handcuffed. And then she forced her body to move. She snatched up her jacket and hurried through the crowd. She left the club and walked down the street, not daring to look back.

But once more, she stopped. Something strange was going on. To her left, rising up behind a fenced-off parking lot was the flank of an enormous building, windowless and covered with posters for concerts, musicals and movies, pasted all the way across and much higher than a person could naturally reach. Identical posters were repeated in clusters, patches of image and text that combined to form some yet undeciphered macro-language, all-inclusive, containing the whole city like a reflection in an enormous compound eye. And then the colors swam, and the whole eye swiveled down to face her, and she stared with awe at the giant eye of the city, colors shimmering, patterns forming and transforming in an overwhelming variety.

Carl caught up to her, panting, and touched her shoulder, a small, thrilling shock to his fingertips.

"You waited again," he said, his voice still hoarse from running.

"I've been dosed," she said.

"What?"

"That bastard overgrown infant. He dosed my drink."

"How do you know?"

"The wall is moving."

Carl stared at the wall, which didn't move at all. He wanted to see what she saw. He looked from her radiant face to the looming wall, noisy with color and shape and language. He tried to see it as she did. He thought of his earlier image of the city, the giant monster that it was. He had presumed he'd beaten it, but it was much stronger than he'd imagined; he'd merely pricked it and now it was howling for revenge. It would devour her. He scrambled for something to say that would alleviate her terrible vision.

"It's the most...." she started to say.

"I'll take you away from this. We'll live on a mountain together and you'll never have to see it again." He watched for her reaction. She was still staring at the wall.

"It's the most...beautiful thing I've ever seen."

She looked at him. She looked right through him. Her eyes were round, teary gems, green with reddened whites.

"It needs me," she said quietly.

"What needs you?"

Laura finally looked at Carl.

"Leave me alone."

"I'll never do that," his voice was mean with exasperation. And then with pain, as she turned away, "*I* need you."

Laura ran, and Carl pursued her through the streets, her boots clicking and his untied sneakers flapping not far behind. She fled west, seeking obscure, sinuous streets, and refuge from the sun·which threatened to rise. And he was never far behind. And the city observed the chase with its countless eyes, eyes of streetlights and headlights' and glinting windows and shards of splintered glass.

She reached the city's edge. She saw the Hudson flowing blackly beyond the city lights, and before it, the dark, empty roadway of the West Side Highway. Hearing his steps, feeling his breath on the nape of her neck, she reached into her jacket pocket, spun around and sprayed him with pepper gas.

He took a few steps past her, staggering into the middle of the broad service road. He sank to his knees, retching and rubbing his eyes. A jet of light streaked along the faces of dark buildings and struck her eyes. A taxi swung around a bend in the road, heading straight for Carl.

She knew instantly what she would do. She had been preparing for this moment for longer than she knew. She would put her own body in its path, this body everyone wanted but her, and solve two problems at once.

She tried to move, but something else happened instead. Her feet took root in the cement on the corner, and her arm stretched out over the street like a gossamer wing. The baubles of her ringed fist blazed in warning, and her red lips formed a silent cry as her body lengthened and hardened and shone with letters and light.

Carl heard the screeching of tires, and the idling of an engine. He winced in the headlights' glare. He struggled to his feet. After a few seconds the cab was in motion again; it honked and swerved around him, gathering speed as it rode out of his life, under a series of floating green lights receding into the distance. He walked to where the cab had stopped for her. He coughed and rubbed his eyes, and to steady himself, he grabbed hold of the green metal gear box of the traffic light on the corner. It was warm and from within he heard a noise. He pressed his ear to the box and listened to the ticking of its mechanical heart. He looked out over the water and then up the roadway again at the traffic lights, evenly spaced for as far as his vision would permit, beacons of safety and order, shining their light for no one on the empty street but him. Soon the traffic would begin, and the lights would guide and shape their hectic flow. Listening to the ticking of the heart he felt his own grow large, big enough to encompass the city whose grandeur he had just begun to comprehend. He knew he would spend the rest of his days here, he could never leave. He looked up at the yellow-cased face of the light, letters shining from the black like constellations in the void, momentous and beautiful, like a proof to validate even the most impossible of longings and hopes.

Walk, it said, but he would not. He would hold on, and wait for the change, at first a trepidatious flicker, but then, for a full minute, absolutely sure.

Dont Walk. Dont Walk. Dont Walk.
Dont Walk.

CITY IN LOVE

She is here, after all, and you realized you knew she would be, you always knew; and you tell her that you knew but never dared to say it, afraid she would not be here, afraid she would be nowhere, and could you have lived through that? but she is here, and there is no more need for shields or barbs, cynicism, scorn, it is time to put them down; and you look back on how solitary your life was before, and you feel a pang of pity for your former self — that was me$_{+15}$, you think, incredulous, another person entirely, hopelessly fragmented, less a being than a living ruin; you look into her eyes and laugh, how absurdly bright, eyes like water$_{+10}$ diamonds, crystal wind and star ice$_{+13}$, that understand you for all the things that could be within you and will be from now on; you hold hands, twine fingers in fingergaps, your hands never felt quite right before and now you know why; her hair swirling in the gray milk sky; she leans back against the low mottled brick wall of the rooftop; you lean toward her; your heads tilt, yours to your right, hers to hers; and then her lips, cool and fragrant, the sensation of a drink of rosewater or intake of spring air like the sound of it whistling in through your parted lips, like the sound of birdsong, or an alarm clock as you wake up alone on a hard bed at the front end of an overcast day. You shut your eyes tight but sleep does not return, while outside the buildings crowd your window and gray light laughs in your face.

You arrive early, a rarity. You stand outside the building, its glass front rising into the sky. There is a woman in love with you. You sit inside your office looking out at the city$_{+14}$ composed of glass and tangled lines$_{+11}$. There is work to be done, a perfume called Desire in need of an image. A sample on your desk, and it smells like the colors of exotic currencies should smell. If there were a perfume called Despair it would smell like offices, cleansers that fail to cut the musk and only add to it, trapped air funneled through lungs of dusty tin where microbes make their bed; last month experts came, building doctors standing by the ventilators, sampling the building's breath. The sickest buildings are those with the greatest insularity$_{+11}$, and in this one building in particular—made entirely$_{+3}$ for the sake of selling back to people their own desires brightly boxed — the sickness may be fitting.

You pick up your pencil. You rest your head on your arm on the desk and stare into the interstice of sketchbook page and hovering tip of lead. There was a stairwell, nacreous, fluorescent, stifling, featureless, and the echo of her footfall from landings above. There was a rooftop, covered with gravel and bits of jagged glass, billowing tarpaulins and ropes, buckets of tar and rusty mushroom vents. And beyond, just a heavy mist (but the city was out there, you somehow know). And she was there. Her blazing hair. Her kiss, the whistle of birds and wind. That sensation$_{+12}$ stronger than anything felt in waking life$_{+9}$.

Like a memory of sunlight, that $love_{+10}$, a love that $burns_{+7}$ away at the fog of your automaton day.

There is a knock at your door. It is your partner, the woman in love with you. She comes in and stands before your desk, waiting for you to speak.

"Good morning," you say.

"Good morning," she says, her daybreak smile.

You put down your pencil, and without lifting your head from your arm, you hold up the bottle of perfume.

"Desire," you say, in a monochrome voice.

"Desire," she says, breathily, one hand fluttering up to rest its back against her upturned forehead. "Desire," she says, and does a little dance, spinning on her toes, other hand holding wide her imaginary flowing gown while the dark skirt of her dress suit hugs her legs. You begin to sketch, thinking about all the offices, all the little rooms in which two partners work, art directors and copywriters, daubing the world each day with a fresh coat of pictures and words to make all the old things slick as new.

"Keep dancing," you say.

She huffs with amused affront. Strikes a few exaggerated poses, watching for your reaction. You are not looking at her but you see her peripherally over the horizon of your page as you sketch two figures on a rooftop, with the city peaking all around. A man with trapezoid torso and broadsword tie, a woman with flowing gown and fluttering scarf, poised statuelike, the blank ovals that would be their faces facing one another. You rip out the sheet and put it aside. She comes over and studies it with her best studious look, creasebrowed.

There was a stairwell, stifling hot, featureless. Almost. Red cases on the walls of the landings.

"A rooftop," she says.

There was a pursuit, and echoes.

"...the city..." she says.

There was a rooftop and mist (or was it fog?)

"...a couple..."

You are sketching the figure of a man walking between narrow walls.

"...lovers..."

You begin to sketch figures on the walls, reflections of the man.

"...a chase," she says. "through a maze of glass, some transparent, some reflective..."

In one of the panes of the maze, you sketch the woman's silhouette.

"...he is lost," she says, "and disconsolate. If only they could touch$_{+8}$. If only they could escape$_{+5}$ these glass walls..."

There were letters in white on the red cases in the almost featureless stairwell.

"...but then he finds a clue..."

You are drawing the figure of the man, holding to his faceless oval a woman's slack scarf.

"...he presses the scarf to his face, and smells the fragrance," she says. "He knows which way to go..."

You place the first drawing next to the last, sketching in the walls around them.

"...and he finds her..."

You draw them from above, the maze around them.

"...and we rise above them, and see them in the middle of the maze, on the rooftop, surrounded by the city..."

You sketch in a vague grid of the city, the peaks of the buildings.

"...as we pull away," she says, "a man's voice: 'The city is in love...'"

You draw the building on which they stand. Shape of the perfume bottle.

"...a woman's voice: 'Desire.'"

The two of you stare at the drawings on the desktop.

You break early for lunch though you are not thinking about food. You are thinking about streets and buildings, about the people like you in offices looking through the windows, looking down at the street, at other windows, the spectacle that surrounds them, this city $where_0$ they can watch a thousand times over their $forms_{+6}$ repeated with slight variations, like an illusion resulting $entirely_{-3}$ from mirrors, $where_0$ images are shuffled and displaced, $endless_{+5}$ reflections that $trap_{+2}$ each other in false spaces...this is what you are thinking as you walk through the midday crowd, if it really can be called thinking, your thoughts to real thoughts as is your route to those of those around you, an imitation, or worse, a parody of purpose.

Ahead of you, facing away, there is a boy searching the sidewalk for something he has lost or something someone else has lost, quarters perhaps, to spend in the arcade up the street. You study that $sorrowful_{+11}$ boy. You $must_{+7}$ be much older than he, but you almost don't believe it. Almost as if you went to sleep one night as a child and the ensuing years passed in a dream, and only now in this moment have you awakened with a suit and a tie and an altitude of six feet. You look down at the terrain of the sidewalk flying by. Adults think of children as being close to the ground, but you remember being a boy and watching the ground as a landscape thousands of feet below. As you pass him you are feeling the change in your pocket, thinking about the space of pockets, how they are always felt, never seen. Feeling the change, thinking what it would feel like to be the change, trapped in that close space, the suffocating heat and nauseous jerking of the leg. You are carried but do not know where, valued but do not know why. You seem to be able to empathize with everyone and everything save yourself, in whose existence you only nominally believe. You are feeling for the boy as well as for the change; and you drop a quarter near the gutter, directly$_{+5}$ in his path, where he could not fail to see$_{+5}$ it.

In this city there is a woman who loves you and she is a copywriter but she aspires to write children's books, and you wonder if this boy would ever read one of them. You doubt it. He spends his miniature life in a room full of television screens, staring into them all day, dreaming about them all night.

You consider entering the arcade but it is for children and you are it seems no longer a child. Just beyond this one is another arcade, for adults. A guy from the media department told you to check it out, days or years ago. You enter and walk toward the back, into a booth where you insert a coin and a metal shutter rises mechanically, revealing a window through which you see a woman masturbating on a circular, rotating bed, her back lifted in an arch supported by her shoulders and feet. As the bed spins her around, you watch between the peaks of her knees and the slopes of her thighs her taut middle finger moving in a circular motion against her sex, which glistens under the lights and churns along with her waxed buttocks in an opposite circular motion, circlings within circlings, like the gearwork of a clock. The bed is surrounded by booths with men, each one_0 immaterial and invisible to others save through the fleeting glimpses $captured_{+4}$ behind the openings and closings of the shutters. Between the shutters are mirrors which reflect at various angles the woman, and other shutters and eyes of men behind glass. You came here to think about women but you find yourself thinking about the apparatus. The momentary apparitions of other voyeurs seem somehow an integral part of the show, a feedback of leering eyes.

You repair to your office and close the door. You rest your head on your arms on the desk. Desire is the word that you say to yourself in the voice inside your head, a voice that sounds like your voice sounds to itself. Desire...soon televisions all over the city $will_0$ reverberate with the $word_{+9}$ in ten million lonely caves, on ten million screens, those false spaces of false $sight_{+6}$ where dreamers live their dreamlives, each one_0 falling alone together into the screen, the chase, the maze, to hear the word that lies therein, the $trap_{-2}$ you $will_0$ have set for them. Desire.

Your partner knocks and comes in and perches on your desk, offers her daybreak smile, crosses her legs smoothly at eye level. She talks about a children's story she is writing, about a $girl_{+4}$ who $spies_{+7}$ on life in all its forms, and becomes whatever she spies. She spies a squirrel and becomes the squirrel and leaps from branch to branch, not once losing her balance. She spies a pelican on the beach and becomes the pelican and launches into the air. She flies, exhilarated, until she becomes hungry (for flying is rather strenuous) and tries to catch a codfish. She folds back her wings and slices through the ocean's shimmering skin cleanly as an arrow. But then she becomes the fish and weaves through the water and it is even better than flying. She happily explores the water, becoming one fish after another, until through the wavering water she spies a boy fishing off a dock. And she falls in love, but she cannot look at him too long or she will become him, which would be a problem.

She is not sure how to end it.

"She shares her power with the boy," you say, "in hopes that they will gaze into each other's eyes, becoming each other endlessly. But the boy is very foolish, and he looks at a flower and becomes the flower, and can never change again because the flower has no eyes."

"And she waters it with her tears," she says, "for she has become a cloud." (handfluttering)

"She can't become a cloud. Living things only." *...behind the glass...*

"It's my story." (amused affront)

"Not really fit for children." *...the screens...*

"You may be right." (studiousbrowed)

"I think I'll take a nap." *...the rooftop...*

"What about Desire?" (the little dance)

"I do my best work in my sleep." *...absurdly bright...*

"...or in bed?" (smoothly crossing)

"...especially...."

You go to many places. The one that stays with you is a bedroom, a bed that thinking back you will not recognize, but one that is for the moment your bed in what is for the moment your room or had been for many years many years ago; there is a woman standing beside the bed, facing away, a woman whom thinking back you will not recognize but whom you for the moment had loved for many years and still love yet have lost many years ago; you reach up for her; you wrap your hands around her waist and press your cheek to her jeans, her backside a pillow; you cannot rise, and so you pull her down into the bed; she is beneath you; you press your lips to her pale neck and to your lips comes warmth and the insistence of a living pulse

and that is when you wake up, and you are no longer in that room you no longer recognize. You realize that you are in the hard bed, the bed that gives berth to you every night, on a gray morning

but you cannot get up because you are awake inside your dream, and you are stifling hot and you need to wake up because you cannot breathe; and you open your eyes a crack and see the gray light under the edge of the pillow that covers your head; and you try to move your hand to move the pillow away, and your hand rises slowly, slowly, but it is not your hand that moves, and these are not your eyes that see the light, and your voice that murmurs is not your voice but the voice in your head that imitates your voice as it sounds to yourself, and you must wake up because hot and cannot breathe, and there is the woman in love with you, and there is work to be done, there is a perfume called

and here you are, lifting your head from your crossed and pinpricking arms and the jacket slides from your head and slips from the desk to the floor.

And you wonder that you felt so urgently the need to escape$_{-5}$ the dream$_{+4}$.

You have passed through another workday and you are sitting on an inclined bench, pressing handles outward against ineluctable inward force. The gym is full; dull weights rise and fall in gleaming frames. People heave the weights, they gaze into the mirrored walls, they breathe in staggered time_{+5}, they find themselves lurking in certain sites_{+3}, here and there, in the middle distances of the mirrors. The worst dreams are those when you wake inside the dream and cannot wake outside.

Side by side with your reflection, but really some way away, a woman cranks in a rowing machine, and a man joggles in a treadmill; as he runs in place_{+4}, he looks at her, his form visible behind hers in the glass_{+3}, while she looks up and sees you looking at him before shifting your eyes to her, and she looks away. Everywhere, eyes like flowers, fragile, hopeful for light. You remember the hot stairwell, featureless save for the red cases and flowers, silver flowers on the ceiling when you looked up to follow the echoes of her footfall from landings above.

There is a woman in love with you and you are walking to meet her for dinner. The day is ending now and the gray light darkens. You hold before you an image of days when the lowering sun is present, unlike now_{+2}, and the glass of the endless_{-5} street burns_{-7} so bright it seems the city is on fire_{+2}. On such days it seems it could go otherwise but today you know how it will go. You know that she will talk and you will not say much, that she will try very hard and you will feel sympathy for her effort, and loathe yourself all the more for your inability to make it much easier for her, lost as you are in the befuddled haze that floats through you on days like these, a haze of insensate particles that on better days might cohere, might carry you along, making of the miasma of street baubles a current of possibilities or even clues. What could be made of what there is? There is an unshaven, youngish man crouched in a recess, tuning a guitar. There is a man with greased hair and a double-breasted suit ignoring a traffic light, cursed by a cabbie. There is a homeless man wheeling a shopping cart full of parti-colored trash, there is the red dusklight dancing in captivity, $captured_{-4}$ in the glass of storefronts and office buildings, there is a $girl_{-4}$ who disappears around a corner and the passing men who watch the space where she was. There is the woman in love with you, up ahead in the sea of $life_{-9}$. She positions herself near a display window $directly_{-5}$ across from the fountain where you have arranged to meet. As you approach, she straightens, and then slouches as if to be casual, and oscillates through a few more increasingly subtle adjustments as she decides how she wants you to see_{-5} her. She settles into a contemplative posture before the patterned array of $water_{-10}$ jetting and bobbling, sheeting and splashing, ever and never the same. You stop and wait for her to look up, which she can't help doing.

She is pixie-formed and child-eyed, looking at you tiltwise with palmcradled cheek, and you are looking at your $forms_{-6}$ recessing into infinity in the abyssal mirrors undoing the $walls_{+3}$.

The waiter positions your food before you. Steam rises in a million distances.

You see your reflections placing their hands over all the candles on all the tables, waiting to feel the pain. You see the reflections of the woman in love with you, startled, moving to save your hand from the fire$_{-2}$. But when she reaches out she is grasping at nothing$_{+3}$. You have already drawn away. She asks you what's wrong. You must$_{-7}$ speak now$_{-2}$ but you don't know what to say, of course. You wonder about her desire$_{+2}$ to touch$_{-8}$ you, you, in whose existence you only nominally believe.

She worries the cut flower peering over the lip of its vase. In the candlelight her face is murkily complected. She is one of those rare people that look better in bright light than dim light. She is beautiful even, in light that is very bright. She is waiting for you to speak. You take a breath, and tell her about your dream, knowing it will only hurt her and not help you in the slightest, but you need to tell it and she is the one you need to tell it to. You tell her about the stairwell, and the glass-fronted cases, and the words you cannot make out, the silver flowers, the echoes of footfall above, the rooftop, the fog, the woman with crystal eyes, prism eyes, mirror eyes, the love you felt.

She has listened, sadly, eyes downturned. She seems to sigh but makes no sound.

"Who is she?" she finally asks, shadow of a voice.

a million shrugs of padded shoulders

"She understands you..."

a million nods of obtuse heads

"...better than anyone else you know..."

a million dark waiters in white

"...maybe she exists, somewhere..."

a million glasses filled with water

"...maybe close by even..."

peering flowers into infinity

In the map of your day you could locate sites$_{-3}$ where reflection creates a haven of insularity$_{-11}$. The subway commute is one of these. You stare at the swinging of the red knob on the short rope and the letters that read Emergency Brake. You hunt back through your dream$_{-4}$ and find$_0$ what it reminds you of: the red cases in the stairwell, glass-fronted and lettering that might have read Fire Case or Case of Fire as you chased the echoes of her footfall from landings above. You try to picture her face, and realize that you can, just as well as women's faces you have actually known, which is to say approximately well, not completely. Her skin a little too pale, eyebrows a little too thin, face wide in the cheekbones, narrow in the chin, mouth a little too small. A face excessively prismatic, but one that should exist. With a touch of dread, you search your memory for analogues to that face, hoping for but also fearing a match, because what if it were someone inaccessible, a famous actress or worse, a museum portrait, centuries out of reach. But you cannot find it anywhere except in the dream image. You wonder if you will ever find$_0$ each other in reality. How can this dream ever be realized$_{+3}$? If only she had spoken. Might you have recognized the voice?

A woman catches your stare and you look away. You realize you have been examining the faces of the women on the train, one by one. You wonder what if eyes cast rays, you picture the lines$_{-11}$ of sight$_{-6}$, the pattern of beams that would evolve, bundling about the more looked-at things, the windows, the doors, the crossed legs of the tall woman in the short skirt, the young couple in the alcove at the front of the car, whispering, moving lips profiled in the light of the next car through the glass$_{-3}$. They are in love$_{-10}$, the imaginary beams of their gazes illuminating each other's eyes and every aspect of their faces. Your eyes are drawn away to the lands of advertisements, so familiarly exotic: a beach with water too blue and a sunbathing woman, below an enormous red and roiling sun, below an airline logo; next to this a beer bottle rising amidst haunting and twisted formations of ice_{-13}, not uncommon, presumably, in such a rarefied locale. Freezing in that $place_{-4}$, and desolate beyond conception.

...fire and ice, side by side...

...fire cases, crystal eyes, stifling heat, water eyes, fog, letters, and glass....

In your apartment, in the dark, you gaze out your window at the darkened windows of houses across the street. You watch as a jewel-eyed white cat on a fire escape $spies_{-7}$ a dreaming boy as he wanders by, and with a shudder comes a $sensation_{-12}$ of a significance you cannot place as you watch him light a book of matches on fire, toss it in a lidless trash can and run away down the block. There is smoke, but it does not seem the fire will catch, and so what if it does? You dismiss the scene and lie down on your hard bed, gazing up at the quadrangle of pale light on the dark ceiling. You remember the boy you saw earlier, scouring the ground for quarters. You feel that there should be a way to make sense of all the things you have witnessed today, that all the things could or should fit together with the help of a faculty other than logic, a process whose very existence has been walled off from you all your life. You look to the bedroom walls. How many walls in the city. More walls than people in the city. The city neurotic with walls. In the city people spend their waking hours hidden within $walls_{-3}$. And this only amplifies to a painful degree the $desire_{-2}$ for open spaces. Mirrors to mitigate, to an extent, this desire.

The city is made of this desire...

...and desire is made of reflections...
...and reflections are made of dreams...
...and dreams are made of love...
...all these waking years, you felt nothing$_{-3}$....

Over time$_{-5}$ though, you came to rely on this lack, a lack that filled you so much it seemed like plenitude.

You are in bed, trying to conjure the dream. You want to think about the woman but it is as if she is a light too bright to look at head on. Instead, you think of the stairwell and the heat, and the red knob and the gazes, and the rooftop and the fog (or was it smoke?), and the shutters and the bed, and the cool drink of lips and birdsong, and the candle and the flower, and the boy and the flower, and the boy and the matches, and the red, glass-fronted cases, and the words in white. And you can make them out now, the words, and it is so simple, for they read In Case Of Fire Break Glass. And the silver flowers on the ceiling of course are sprinklers. In the case of fire and the breaking of the glass of the case, an alarm would sound perhaps, and the water would flow from the sprinklers and the fire would be quenched, of course, but meaning what? and you are nudged by the ringing of the phone beside your bed.

A voice you know, the woman in love with you. Distant voice. Nothing but voice. And you struggle to sound your own, mustering only a whisper.

"...barely awake..." you say.

"At dinner tonight...."

"...tonight...?"

"You seemed so troubled."

"...troubled...?"

"I was worried."

"...worried...?"

"How could you not have realized$_{-3}$? I'll tell you
— yes, you are that sorrowful$_{-11}$ sometimes and I can't
help but worry about you."

You are drifting off to sleep. In your ear, there are echoes,
a voice telling you a children's story that blends in and out of
your sleepbound reflections on the day. You are half listening
to the words, word after word$_{-9}$, and you might fear the
reflections$_0$ will be unmade by means of those ech-
oes$_0$, but in time, the reflections$_0$ will be only further
knotted by means of those echoes$_0$ in this nacreous space$_0$
of your mind, intensifying the trance you are in.* The voice is
telling you a story that goes "In a city$_{-14}$...

...space$_0$ of the city, and will bring it crashing down in
a shower of glass. All you have to do is say the word. Say who
it is, the lover of your dreams. Say it, with your wakeful voice,
strong and clear, and wake from the futile dream, no longer
alone, into daybreak. Who is it? Shall I give you a hint?"

In your inner ear you hear the whispered word; and
you say the word; but is it your voice, or the voice that's not
your voice, when the word you say is... me$_{-15}$?

...poor you$_0$, so close to free....

---

* To listen to the voice in your ear, return to the footnote star above and
continue reading until you arrive at the highlighted word, "city." Then,
holding what you have read so far suspended in your mind, search for the
other place where "city" appears highlighted (fourteen pages back, as the
subscript number indicates). Then, continue reading from that other place,
until you come to the next highlighted word ("lines"). Then search for
that word's highlighted twin and so on. (Thus, "In a city composed of
glass and tangled lines of sight, where dreamers live...")
You may begin now.

The stories in *City in Love* are based on the transformation myths of Ovid's *Metamorphoses*. For those interested in looking up the myths, the primary correspondences are as follows:

 Perennial

Books by Alex Shakar:

CITY IN LOVE
The New York Metamorphoses
ISBN 0-06-050883-3 (paperback)

In this collection of short stories, his debut work of fiction, Alex Shakar unveils a landscape at once raptly mythological and savagely familiar. Using as his foundation the *Metamorphoses of Ovid*, written at the dawn of the first millennium and seen by many as the shadow Bible of Western civilization, Shakar combines profound literary innovation with humanity, humor, and a heart-stopping lyric sensibility.

City in Love shows us that the way we feel about our urban environment may be increasingly similar to the way the ancients felt about nature— a feeling which gave rise to myth, both in explanation and as an expression of wonder, awe, and the very impossibility of explanation.

"Shakar is an author unafraid to take risks, and when this is combined with genuine talent, the result can be breathtaking."—*American Book Review*

"All of the characters in the collection are recognizably human, striving to be more than human; what a refreshing contrast to the de riguer solipsism of contemporary fiction's urban dwellers."

—*Review of Contemporary American Fiction*

THE SAVAGE GIRL
ISBN 0-06-093523-5 (paperback)
A *NEW YORK TIMES* NOTABLE BOOK

At once a riveting story of two sisters' journey through the highs and lows of postmodern culture and a brilliant exploration of the effects of consumerism on individuals and society as a whole.

"An exceptionally smart and likable first novel that tries valiantly to ransom Beauty from its commercial captors." —Jonathan Franzen

"It is exciting to meet a novelist who isn't afraid of heights."
—*New York Times Book Review*

Available wherever books are sold, or call 1-800-331-3761 to order.